**"Will you marry me, Rebekah?"
Joshua asked.**

"But why?" Her cheeks turned to fire as she added, "That sounded awful. I'm sorry. The truth is you've always been a *gut* friend, Joshua, which is why I feel I can be blunt."

"If we can't speak honestly now, I can't imagine when we could."

"Then I will honestly say I don't understand why you'd ask me to m-m-marry you." She hated how she stumbled over the simple word.

No, it wasn't simple. There was nothing simple about Joshua Stoltzfus appearing at her door to ask her to become his wife.

"Because we could help each other. Isn't that what a husband and wife are? Helpmeets?" He cleared his throat. "I would rather marry a woman I know and respect as a friend. We've both married once for love, and we've both lost the one we love. Is it wrong to be more practical this time?"

Every inch of her wanted to shout, *"Ja!"* But his words made sense.

She'd been blinded by love once. How much better would it be to marry with her eyes wide open?

She'd be a fool not to agree immediately.

Jo Ann Brown has always loved stories with happy-ever-after endings. A former military officer, she is thrilled to have the chance to write stories about people falling in love. She is also a photographer, and she travels with her husband of more than thirty years to places where she can snap pictures. They live in Nevada with three children and a spoiled cat. Drop her a note at joannbrownbooks.com.

Books by Jo Ann Brown

Love Inspired

Amish Hearts

Amish Homecoming
An Amish Match

Love Inspired Historical

Matchmaking Babies

Promise of a Family
Family in the Making
Her Longed-For Family

Sanctuary Bay

The Dutiful Daughter
A Hero for Christmas
A Bride for the Baron

An Amish Match

Jo Ann Brown

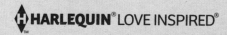

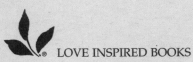

LOVE INSPIRED BOOKS

ISBN-13: 978-0-373-71951-8

An Amish Match

Copyright © 2016 by Jo Ann Ferguson

www.Harlequin.com

Printed in U.S.A.

Have not I commanded thee? Be strong and of a good courage; be not afraid, neither be thou dismayed: for the Lord thy God is with thee whithersoever thou goest.

—*Joshua 1:9*

For Linda Parisi
A dear friend who always makes me smile
just thinking of her

Chapter One

Paradise Springs
Lancaster County, Pennsylvania

The rainy summer afternoon was as dismal as the hearts of those who had gathered at the cemetery. Most of the mourners were walking back to their buggies, umbrellas over their heads like a parade of black mushrooms. The cemetery with its identical stones set in almost straight lines on the neatly trimmed grass was edged by a worn wooden rail fence. The branches on a single ancient tree on the far side of the cemetery rocked with the wind that lashed rain on the few people remaining by the newly covered grave.

Rebekah Burkholder knew she should leave the Stoltzfus family in private to mourn their loss, but she remained to say a silent prayer over the fresh earth. Rose Mast Stoltzfus had been her first cousin, and as *kinder* they'd spent hours together every week doing their chores and exploring the fields, hills and creeks near their families' farms. Now Rose, two years younger than Rebekah, was dead from a horrific asthma attack at twenty-four.

The whole Stoltzfus family encircled the grave where a stone would be placed in a few weeks. Taking a step back, Rebekah tightened her hold on both her son's hand and her umbrella that danced in the fickle wind. Sammy, who would be three in a few months, watched everything with two fingers stuck in his mouth. She knew that over the next few days she would be bombarded with questions—as she had been when his *daed* died. She hoped she'd be better prepared to answer this time. At least she could tell him the truth rather than skirt it because she didn't want him ever to know what sort of man his *daed* had been.

"It's time to go, Sammy," she said in little more than a whisper when he didn't move.

"Say bye-bye?" He looked up at her with his large blue eyes that were his sole legacy from her. He had Lloyd's black hair and apple-round cheeks instead of the red curls she kept restrained beneath her *kapp* and the freckles scattered across her nose and cheeks.

"Ja." She bent to hug him, shifting so her expanding belly didn't bump her son. Lloyd hadn't known about his second *kind* because he'd died before she was certain she was pregnant again. "We have said bye-bye."

"Go bye-bye?"

Her indulgent smile felt out of place at the graveside. Yet, as he had throughout his young life, her son gave her courage and a reason to go on.

"Ja."

Standing slowly because her center of balance changed every day, she held out her hand to him again.

He put his fingers back in his mouth, glanced once more at the grave, then stepped away from it along with her.

Suddenly the wind yanked on Rebekah's umbrella, turning it inside out. As the rain struck them, Sammy pressed his face against her skirt. She fought to hold on to the umbrella. Even the smallest things scared him; no wonder after what he had seen and witnessed in those horrible final months of his *daed*'s life.

No! She would not think of that time again. She didn't want to remember any of it. Lloyd had died last December, almost five months ago, and he couldn't hurt her or their *kinder* again.

"Mamm," Sammy groaned as he clung to her.

"It's all right," she cooed as she tried to fix her umbrella.

She didn't look at any of the other mourners as she forced her umbrella down to her side where the wind couldn't grab it again. Too many people had told her that she mollycoddled her son, and he needed to leave his babyish ways behind now that he was almost three. They thought she was spoiling him because he had lost his *daed*, but none of those people knew Sammy had experienced more fear and despair in his short life than they had in their far longer ones.

"Here. Let me help," said a deep voice from her left.

She tilted her head to look past the brim of her black bonnet. Her gaze rose and rose until it met Joshua Stoltzfus's earth-brown eyes through the pouring rain. He was almost six feet tall, almost ten inches taller than she was. His dark brown hair was damp beneath his black hat that dripped water off its edge. His beard was plastered to the front of the coat he wore to church Sundays, and soaked patches were even more ebony on the wide shoulders of his coat. He'd gotten drenched while helping to fill in the grave.

"Take this," he said, holding his umbrella over her head. "I'll see if I can repair yours."

"Danki." She held the umbrella higher so it was over his head, as well. She hoped Joshua hadn't seen how she flinched away when he moved his hand toward her. Recoiling away from a man's hand was a habit she couldn't break.

"Mamm!" Sammy cried. "I wet now!"

Before she could pull her son back under the umbrella's protection, Joshua looked to a young girl beside him, "Deborah, can you take Samuel under your umbrella while I fix Rebekah's?"

Deborah, who must have been around nine or ten, had the same dark eyes and hair as Joshua. Her face was red from where she'd rubbed away tears, but she smiled as she took Sammy's hand. *"Komm.* It's dry with me."

He didn't hesitate, surprising Rebekah. He usually waited for permission before he accepted any invitation. Perhaps, at last, he realized he didn't have to ask now that Lloyd was dead.

Joshua turned her umbrella right side out, but half of it hung limply. The ribs must have been broken by the gust.

"Danki," she said. "It's *gut* enough to get me to our buggy."

"Don't be silly." He tucked the ruined umbrella under his left arm and put his hand above hers on the handle of his umbrella.

Again she flinched, and he gave her a puzzled look. Before she could let go, his fingers slid down to cover hers, holding them to the handle.

"We'll go with you back to your buggy," he said.

She didn't look at him because she didn't want to see his confusion. How could she explain to Lloyd's best friend about her reaction that had become instinctive? "I don't want to intrude on…" She gulped, unable to go on as she glanced at the other members of the Stoltzfus family by the grave.

"It's no intrusion. I told *Mamm* we'd go back to the house to make sure everything was ready for those gathering there."

She suspected he wasn't being completely honest. The *Leit*, the members of their church district, would oversee everything so the family need not worry about any detail of the day. However, she was grateful for his kindness. She'd always admired that about him, especially when she saw him with one of his three *kinder*.

Glancing at the grave, she realized neither of his boys remained. Timothy, who must have been around sixteen, had already left with his younger brother, Levi, who was a year older than Deborah.

"Ready to go?" Joshua asked as he tugged gently on the umbrella handle and her hand.

"Ja." Instantly she changed her mind. "No."

Stepping away, she was surprised when he followed to keep the umbrella over her head. She appreciated staying out of the rain as she walked to Isaiah, her cousin's widower. The young man who couldn't yet be thirty looked as haggard as a man twice his age as he stared at the overturned earth. Some sound must have alerted him, because he turned to see her and his older brother coming toward him.

Rebekah didn't speak as she put her hand on Isaiah's black sleeve. So many things she longed to say, because from everything she had heard the newlyweds had been deeply in love. They would have celebrated their first anniversary in November.

All she could manage to say was, "I'm sorry, Isaiah. Rose will be missed."

"*Danki*, Rebekah." He looked past her to his oldest brother. "Joshua?"

"Rebekah's umbrella broke," Joshua said simply. "I'm walking her to her buggy. We'll see you back at the house."

Isaiah nodded but said nothing more as he turned to look at the grave.

Joshua gripped his brother's shoulder in silent commiseration, then motioned for Rebekah to come with him. As soon as they were out of earshot of the remaining mourners, he said, "It was very kind. What you said to Isaiah."

"I don't know if he really heard me or not. At Lloyd's funeral, people talked to me but I didn't hear much other than a buzz like a swarm of bees."

"I remember feeling that way, too, when my Matilda died." He steered her around a puddle in the grass. "Even though we had warning as she sickened, nothing could ease my heart when she breathed her last."

"She was blessed to have you with her until the end." She once had believed she and Lloyd could have such a love. Would she have been as caring if Lloyd had been ill instead of dying because he'd fallen from the hayloft in a drunken stupor?

No! She wasn't going to think about that awful moment again, a moment when only her faith had kept her from giving in to panic. The certainty that God would hold her up through the horrible days ahead had allowed her to move like a sleepwalker through the following month. Her son and the discovery she was pregnant again had pulled her back into life. Her *kinder* needed her, and she wouldn't let them down any longer. It was important that nobody know the truth about Lloyd, because she didn't want people watching Sammy, looking for signs that he was like his *daed*.

"I know Rose's death must be extra hard for you," Joshua murmured beneath the steady thump of rain on his umbrella, "because it's been barely half a year since you buried Lloyd. My Matilda has been gone for more than four years, and the grief hasn't lessened. I've simply become accustomed to it, but the grief is still new for you."

She didn't answer.

He glanced down at her, his brown eyes shadowed, but his voice filled with compassion. "I know how much I miss Lloyd. He was my best friend from our first day of school. But nothing compares with losing a spouse, especially a *gut* man like Lloyd Burkholder."

"That's true." But, for her, mourning was not sad in the way Joshua described his own.

Lloyd Burkholder had been a *gut* man…when he'd been sober. As he had never been drunk beyond their home, nobody knew about how a *gut* man became a cruel man as alcohol claimed him. The teasing about how she was clumsy, the excuse she gave for the bruises and her broken finger, hurt almost as much as his fist had.

She put her hand over her distended belly. Lloyd would never be able to endanger their second *kind* as he had his first. Now she wouldn't have to worry about doing everything she could to avoid inciting his rage, which he'd, more than once, aimed at their unborn *kind* the last time she was pregnant. Before Sammy was born, she'd been fearful Lloyd's blows might have damaged their *boppli*. God had heard her desperate prayers because Sammy was perfect when he was born, and he was growing quickly and talking nonstop.

Joshua started to say more, then closed his mouth. She understood. Too many sad memories stood between them, but there were *gut* ones, as well. She couldn't deny that. On the days when Lloyd hadn't been drunk, he had often taken her to visit Joshua and Matilda. Those summery Sunday afternoons spent on the porch of Joshua and Matilda's comfortable white house while they'd enjoyed iced tea had been *wunderbaar*. They had ended when Matilda became ill and was diagnosed with brain cancer.

A handful of gray buggies remained by the cemetery's gate. The horses had their heads down as rain pelted them, and Rebekah guessed they were as eager to return to their dry stalls and a *gut* rubdown as Dolly, her black buggy horse, was.

"Mamm!" Sammy's squeal of delight sounded out of place in the cemetery.

She whirled to see him running toward them. Every possible inch of him was wet, and his clothes were covered with mud. Laughter bubbled up from deep inside her. She struggled to keep it from bursting out.

When she felt Joshua shake beside her, she discovered he was trying to restrain his own amusement. She looked quickly away. If their gazes met, even for a second, she might not be able to control her laughter.

"Whoa!" Joshua said, stretching out a long arm to keep Sammy from throwing himself against Rebekah. "You don't want to get your *mamm* dirty, do you?"

"Dirty?" the toddler asked, puzzled.

Deborah came to a stop right behind Sammy. "I tried

to stop him." Her eyes filled with tears again. "But he jumped into the puddle before I could."

Rebekah pulled a cloth out from beneath her cape. She'd pinned it there for an emergency like this. Wiping her son's face, she gave the little girl a consoling smile. "Don't worry. He does this sort of thing a lot. I hope he didn't splash mud on you."

"He missed me." The girl's smile returned. "I learned how to move fast from being around *Aenti* Ruth's *kinder*. I wish I could have been fast enough to keep him from jumping in the puddle in the first place."

"No one is faster than a boy who wants to play in the water." Joshua surprised her by winking at Sammy. "Isn't that right?"

Her son's smile vanished, and he edged closer to Rebekah. He kept her between Joshua and himself. Her yearning to laugh disappeared. Her son didn't trust any man, and he had *gut* reason not to. His *daed*, the man he should have been able to trust most, could change from a jovial man to a brutal beast for no reason a toddler could comprehend.

"Let's get you in the buggy." Joshua's voice was strained, and his dark brown eyes narrowed as he clearly tried to understand why Sammy would shy away from him in such obvious fear.

She wished she could explain, but she didn't want to add to Joshua's grief by telling him the truth about the man her husband truly had been.

"Hold this," he said as he ducked from under the umbrella. Motioning for his daughter to take Sammy's hand again, he led them around the buggy. Rain struck him, but he paid no attention. He opened the door on the passenger side. "You probably want to put something on the seat to protect the fabric."

"*Danki*, Joshua. That's a *gut* idea." She stretched forward to spread the dirty cloth on the seat. She shouldn't be surprised that he was concerned about the buggy, because he worked repairing and making buggies not far from his home in Paradise Springs. She stepped back while Joshua swung her son up into the carriage. If he noticed how Sammy stiffened, he didn't say anything.

Once Sammy was perched on the seat with his two fingers firmly in his mouth, Joshua drew the passenger side door closed and made sure it was latched so her son couldn't open it and tumble out. He took his daughter's hand before they came back to stand beside her.

Rebekah raised the umbrella to keep the rain off them. When he grasped the handle, she relinquished it to him, proud that she had managed not to shrink away. He smiled tautly, then offered his hand to assist her into the buggy.

"Be careful," he warned as if she were no older than her son. "The step up is slick, and you don't want to end up as muddy as Samuel."

"You're right." She appreciated his attempt to lighten her spirits as much as she did his offer.

Placing her hand on his palm, she bit her lower lip as his broad fingers closed over it. She'd expected his hands to be as chilled as hers, but they weren't. Warmth seeped past the thick wall she'd raised to keep others from discovering what a fool she'd been to marry Lloyd Burkholder.

Quickly she climbed into the buggy. Joshua didn't hold her hand longer than was proper. Yet the gentle heat of his touch remained, a reminder of how much she'd distanced herself from everyone else in their community.

"*Danki,* Joshua." She lowered her eyes, which were oddly almost even with his as she sat on the buggy seat. "I keep saying that, but I'm truly grateful for your help." She smiled at Deborah. "*Danki* to you, too. You made Sammy giggle, and I appreciate that."

"He's fun," she said, waving to him before running to another buggy farther along the fence.

"We'll see you back at *Mamm'*s house," Joshua said as he unlashed the reins and handed them to her.

She didn't say anything one way or the other. She could use her muddy son as an excuse not to spend the afternoon with the other mourners, but she didn't want to be false with Joshua, who had always treated her with respect and goodness. Letting him think she'd be there wasn't right, either. She stayed silent.

"Drive carefully," he added before he took a step back.

Unexpected tears swelled in her eyes, and she closed the door on her side. When they were first married, Lloyd had said that to her whenever she left the farm. He'd stopped before the end of their second month as man and wife. Like so much else about him, she hadn't known why he'd halted, even when he was sober.

It felt *wunderbaar* to hear a man use those commonplace words again.

"Go?" asked her son, cutting through her thoughts.

"*Ja.*" She steered the horse onto the road after looking back to make sure Joshua or someone else wasn't driving past. With the battery operated lights and windshield wiper working, she edged the buggy's wheels onto the wet asphalt. She didn't want to chance them getting stuck in the mud along the shoulder. In this weather it would take them almost an hour to reach their farm beyond Bird-in-Hand.

Sammy put his dirty hand on her cape. "That man was mad at me."

"Why do you think so?" she asked, surprised. From what she'd seen, Joshua had been nothing but friendly with her son.

"His eyes were funny. One went down while the other stayed up."

It took her a full minute to realize her son was describing Joshua's wink. Pain pierced her heart, which, no matter how she'd tried, refused to harden completely. Her darling *kind* didn't understand what a wink was because there had been too few cheerful times in his short life.

She had to find a way to change that. No matter what. Her *kinder* were the most important parts of her world, and she would do whatever she must to make sure they had a *gut* life from this day forward.

Joshua walked into the farmhouse's large but cozy kitchen and closed the back door behind him, glad to be inside where the unseasonable humidity didn't make everything stick to him. He'd waved goodbye to the last of the mourners who'd came to the house for a meal after the funeral. Their buggy was already vanishing into the night by the time he reached the house.

He was surprised to see only his younger sister Esther and *Mamm* there. Earlier, their neighbors, Leah Beiler and her *mamm*, had helped serve food and collected dishes, which they'd piled on the long table in the middle of the simple kitchen. They had insisted on helping because his older sister Ruth was having a difficult pregnancy, and her family had gone home hours ago.

The thought of his pregnant sister brought Rebekah to mind. Even though she was going to have a *boppli*, too, she had no one to help her on the farm Lloyd had left her. He wondered again why she hadn't joined the mourners at his *mamm*'s house. Being alone in the aftermath of a funeral was wrong, especially when she'd suffered such a loss herself.

Take care of her, Lord, he prayed silently. *Her need is great at this time.*

A pulse of guilt rushed through him. Why hadn't he considered that before? Though it was difficult to see her because she brought forth memories of her late husband and Matilda, that was no excuse to turn his back on her.

Tomorrow, he promised himself. Tomorrow he would go to her farm and see exactly what help she needed. The trip would take him a long way from his buggy shop in Paradise Springs, but he'd neglected his obligations to Lloyd's wife too long. Maybe she would explain why she'd pulled away, her face growing pale each time he came near. He couldn't remember her acting like that before Lloyd died.

"Everyone's gone." Joshua hung his black hat on the peg by the door and went to the refrigerator. He poured himself a glass of lemonade. He'd forgotten what dusty work feeding, milking and cleaning up after cows could be.

And hungry work. He picked up a piece of ham from the plate on the counter. It was the first thing he'd eaten all day, in spite of half the women in the *Leit* insisting he take a bite of this casserole or that cake. They didn't hide the fact they believed a widower with three *kinder* must never eat a *gut* meal.

"*Mamm*, will you please sit and let me clear the table?" Esther frowned and put her hands on the waist of her black dress.

"I want to help." Their *mamm*'s voice was raspy because she'd talked so much in the past few days greeting mourners, consoling her family and Rose's, and talking with friends. She glowered at the cast on her left arm.

The day before Rose died, *Mamm* had slipped on her freshly mopped floor and stumbled against the table. Hard. Both bones in her lower left arm had broken, requiring a trip to the medical clinic in Paradise Springs. She'd come home with a heavy cast from the base of her fingers to above her elbow, as well as a jar of calcium tablets to strengthen her bones.

"I know, but..." Esther squared her shoulders. "*Mamm*, it's taking me exactly twice as long to do a task because I have to keep my eye on you to make sure you *don't* do it."

"There must be something I can do."

Joshua gave his younger sister a sympathetic smile as he poured a second glass of lemonade. *Mamm* wasn't accustomed to sitting, but she needed to rest her broken arm. Balancing the second glass in the crook of one arm, he gently put his hand on *Mamm*'s right shoulder and guided her to the front room that some of the mourners had put back in order before they'd left. The biggest space in the house, it was where church Sunday services were held once a year when it was *Mamm*'s turn to host them. Fortunately that had happened in the spring, because she was in no state now to invite in the whole congregation.

He felt his *mamm* tremble beneath his fingers, so he reached to open the front door. He didn't want to pause in this big room. It held too many sad memories because it was where his *daed* had been waked years ago.

Not wanting to linger, he steered his *mamm* out on

the porch. He assisted her to one of the rocking chairs before he sat on the porch swing. It squeaked as it moved beneath him. He'd try to remember to oil it before he headed home in the morning to his place about a mile down the road.

"Is Isaiah asleep already?" he asked. "When I was coming in, I saw the light go out in the room where he used to sleep upstairs."

"I doubt he's asleep, though it would be the best thing for him. You remember how difficult it is to sleep after…" She glanced toward the barn.

His other brothers should be returning to the house soon, but he guessed *Mamm* was thinking of the many times she'd watched *Daed* cross the grass between the barn and the house. Exactly as he'd looked out the window as if Matilda would come in with a basket of laundry or fresh carrots and peas from her garden. Now he struggled to keep up with the wash and the garden had more weeds than vegetables.

Mamm sighed. "What are you going to do, Joshua?"

"Do?"

"You need to find someone to watch Levi and Deborah during the day while you're at the shop."

It was his turn to sigh into his sweaty glass. "I'm not sure. The *kinder* loved spending time with Rose, and it's going to be hard for them to realize she won't be watching them again."

"Those who have gone before us keep an eye on us always." She gave him a tremulous smile. "But as far as the *kinder*, I can—"

He shook his head. "No, you can't have them come here. Not while you've got a broken arm. And don't suggest Esther. She'll be doubly busy taking care of the house while you're healing. The doctor said it would take at least six weeks for your bones to knit, and I can't have the *kinder* at the shop for that long."

Levi and Deborah would want to help. As Esther had said to *Mamm*, such assistance made every job take twice as long as necessary. In addition, he couldn't work beneath a buggy, making a repair or putting it together, and keep an eye on them. Many of the tools at the buggy shop were dangerous if mishandled.

"There is an easy solution, Joshua."

"What?"

"Get yourself a wife."

His eyes were caught by the flash of lightning from beyond the tree line along the creek. The stars were vanishing, one after another, as clouds rose high in the night sky. Thunder was muted by the distance, but it rolled across the hills like buggy wheels on a rough road. A stronger storm than the one that morning would break the humidity and bring in fresher air.

Looking back at his *mamm*, he forced a smile. "Get a wife like that?" He snapped his fingers. "And my problems are solved?"

"Matilda died four years ago." Her voice was gentle, and he guessed the subject was as hard for her to speak about as it was for him to listen to. "Your *kinder* have been without a *mamm*, and you've been without a wife. Don't you want more *kinder* and the company of a woman in your home?"

Again he was saved from having to answer right away by another bolt of lightning cutting through the sky. "Looks like the storm is coming fast."

"Not as fast as you're changing the subject to avoid answering me."

He never could fool *Mamm*, and he usually didn't try. On the other hand, she hadn't been trying to match him with some woman before now.

"All right, *Mamm*. I'll answer your question. When the time is right, I may remarry again. The time hasn't been right, because I haven't found the right woman." He drained his lemonade and set the glass beside him. "From your expression, however, I assume you have someone specific in mind."

"*Ja*. I have been thinking about one special person, and seeing you with Rebekah Burkholder today confirmed it for me. She needs a husband."

"Rebekah?" He couldn't hide his shock as *Mamm* spoke of the woman who had remained on his mind since he'd left the cemetery.

"*Ja*, Rebekah. With a young son and a *boppli* coming soon, she can't handle Lloyd's farm on her own. She needs to marry before she has to sell out and has no place to go." *Mamm* shifted, then winced as she readjusted her broken arm. "You know her well, Joshua. She is the widow of your best friend."

That was true. Lloyd Burkholder had been his best friend. When Joshua had married Matilda, Lloyd had served as one of his *Newehockers*, the two male and two female attendants who sat beside the bride and groom throughout their wedding day. It was an honor to be asked, and Lloyd had been thrilled to accept.

"Rebekah is almost ten years younger than I am, *Mamm*."

"Lloyd was your age."

"And she is barely ten years older than Timothy."

"True. That might have made a difference years ago, but now you are adults with *kinder*. And you need a wife."

"I don't need a wife right now. I need someone to watch the *kinder*." He held up his hand. "And Rebekah lives too far away for me to ask her to do that."

"What about the housework? The laundry? The cooking? Rose did much of those chores for you, and you eat your other meals here. Deborah can do some of the work, but not all of it. With Esther having to do my chores as well as her own around the house and preparations for the end of the school year, she would appreciate having fewer people at the table each night."

"*Mamm*, I doubt that," he replied with a laugh, though he knew his sister worked hard at their local school.

His *mamm* wagged a finger at him. "True, true. Esther would gladly feed anyone who showed up every night." As quickly as she'd smiled, she became serious again. "But it's also true Rebekah Burkholder needs a husband. That poor woman can't manage on her own."

He didn't want to admit his own thoughts had gone in that direction, too, and how guilty he felt that he'd turned his back on her.

His face must have betrayed his thoughts because *Mamm* asked, "Will you at least think of it?"

"*Ja.*"

What else could he say? Rebekah likely had no interest in remarrying so quickly after Lloyd's death, but if she didn't take another husband, she could lose Lloyd's legacy to her and his *kinder*. The idea twisted in Joshua's gut.

It was time for him to decide exactly what he was willing to do to help his best friend's widow.

Chapter Two

Even as Joshua was turning his buggy onto the lane leading to the Burkholders' farm the next morning, he fought his own yearning to turn around and leave at the buggy's top speed. He hadn't slept last night, tossing and turning and seeking God's guidance while the loud thunderstorm had banished the humidity. A cool breeze had rushed into the rooms where his three *kinder* had been lost in their dreams, but he had been awake until dawn trying to decide what he should do.

Or, to be more accurate, to accept what he should do. *God never promised life would be simple.* That thought echoed through his head during breakfast and as he prepared for the day.

Into his mind came the verse from Psalm 118 that he had prayed so many times since his wife died. *This is the day which the Lord hath made; we will rejoice and be glad in it.*

At sunrise on this crisp morning, he'd arranged for the younger two *kinder* to go to the Beilers' house, but he couldn't take advantage of their generosity often. Abram Beiler suffered from Parkinson's disease, and Leah and her *mamm* had to keep an eye on him as he went about his chores. Even though Leah had told Joshua to depend on her help for as long as he needed because Leah's niece Mandy and Deborah were close in age and enjoyed playing together, he must find a more permanent solution.

His next stop had been to drop off Timothy at his buggy shop at the Stoltzfus Family Shops in the village. The other shops as well as the smithy behind the long building were run by his brothers. He asked the sixteen-year-old to wait on any customers who came in and to let them know Joshua would be there by midday. Even a year ago, he could have trusted Timothy to sort out parts or paint sections of wood that were ready to be assembled, but his older son had grown less reliable in recent months. Joshua tried to give him space and privacy to sort out the answers every teenager wrestled with, which was why he hadn't said anything when he'd noticed Timothy had a portable music device and earphones hidden beneath his shirt.

Until he decided to be baptized and join the church, Timothy could have such items, though many members of the *Leit* frowned on their use at any age. Most *kinder* chose to be baptized, though a few like Leah's twin brother turned their backs on the community and left to seek a different life among the *Englischers*.

He stopped the family buggy, which was almost twice the size of the one Rebekah had driven away from the cemetery yesterday. Looking out the front, he appraised the small white house. He hadn't been here since at least three years before Matilda died. Only now did he realize how odd it was that they had seldom visited the Burkholders' house.

The house was in poor shape. Though the yard was

neat and flowers had been planted by the front door, paint was chipped on the clapboards and the roof resembled a swaybacked horse. He frowned when he noticed several bricks had fallen off the chimney and tumbled partway down the shingles. Even from where he sat, he could see broken and missing shingles.

What had happened? This damage couldn't have happened in the five months since Lloyd's death. It must have taken years of neglect to bring the house to such a miserable state.

He stroked his beard thoughtfully as he looked at the barn and the outbuildings. They were in a little bit better shape, but not much. One silo was leaning at a precarious angle away from the barn, and a strong wind could topple it. A tree had fallen on a section of the fence. Its branches were bare and the trunk was silvery-gray, which told him it had been lying in the sunshine for several seasons.

Why had Lloyd let his house and buildings deteriorate like this?

Joshua reminded himself he wasn't going to learn any answers sitting in his buggy. After getting out, he lashed the reins around a nearby tree and left his buggy horse Benny to graze on the longer grass at the edge of the driveway. He walked up the sloping yard to the back door. As he looked beyond the barn, he saw two cows in the pasture. Not enough to keep the farm going unless Rebekah was making money in other ways, like selling eggs or vegetables at one of the farmers' markets near the tourist areas.

He knocked on the back door and waited for an answer. The door didn't have a window like his kitchen door, but he could hear soft footsteps coming toward him.

Rebekah opened the door and stared at him, clearly astonished at his unannounced visit in the middle of a workday morning.

He couldn't help staring back. Yesterday her face had been half hidden beneath her bonnet, and he'd somehow pushed out of his mind how beautiful she was. Her deep auburn hair was hidden beneath a scarf she'd tied at her nape. A splotch of soap suds clung to her right cheek and sparkled as brightly as her blue eyes. Her freckles looked as if someone had blown cinnamon across her nose and high cheekbones. There was something ethereal about her when she looked up at him, her eyes wide and her lips parted in surprise. Her hand was protectively on her belly. Damp spots littered the apron she wore over her black dress. He wasn't surprised her feet were bare. *Mamm* and his sisters preferred to go without shoes when cleaning floors.

Then he noticed the gray arcs beneath her eyes and how drawn her face was. Exhaustion. It was the first description that came to mind.

She put her hand to the scarf. "I didn't expect company."

"I know, but it's long past time I paid you and the boy a visit."

For a moment he thought she'd argue, then she edged back and opened the door wider. "Joshua, *komm* in. How is Isaiah?"

"He was still asleep when I went over there this morning." Guilt twinged in him. He'd been so focused on his own problems that he hadn't been praying for his brother's grieving heart. *God, forgive me for being selfish. I need to be there to hold my brother up at this sad time. I know, too well, the emptiness he is feeling today.*

"How's your *mamm*? I have been praying for her to heal quickly."

He stepped into a kitchen that was as neat as the outside of the house was a mess. The tempting scents of freshly made bread and whatever chicken she was cooking on top of the stove for the midday meal teased him to ask her for a sample. When Lloyd and she had come over to his house, she'd always brought cookies or cake, which rivaled the very best he'd ever tasted.

You wouldn't have to eat your own cooking or Deborah's burned meals any longer if Rebekah agrees to marry you, so ask her.

He wished that voice in his head would be quiet. This was tough enough without being nagged by his own thoughts.

Taking off his straw hat and holding it by the brim, Joshua slowly turned it around and around. "*Danki* for asking. *Mamm* is doing as well as can be expected. You know she's not one for sitting around. She's already figuring out what she can do with one hand."

"I'm not surprised." She gave him a kind smile. "Will you sit down? I've got coffee and hot water for tea. Would you like a cup?"

"*Danki*, Rebekah. Tea sounds *gut*," he said as he set his hat on a peg by the door. He pulled out one of the chairs by the well-polished oak table.

"Coming up." She crossed the room to the large propane stove next to the refrigerator that operated on the same fuel.

"*Mamm?*" came her son's voice from the front room. It was followed by the little boy rushing into the kitchen. He skidded to a halt and gawped at Joshua before running to grab Rebekah's skirt.

She put a loving hand on Sammy's dark curls. "You remember Joshua, right?"

He heard a peculiar tension underlying her question and couldn't keep from recalling how Sammy had been skittish around him at the cemetery. Some *kinder* were shy with adults. He'd need to be patient while he gave the boy a chance to get to know him better.

Joshua smiled at the toddler. It seemed as if only yesterday his sons, Timothy and Levi, were no bigger than little Samuel. How sweet those days had been when his sons had shadowed him and listened to what he could share with them! As soon as Deborah was able to toddle, she'd joined them. They'd had fun together while he'd let them help with small chores around the buggy shop and on the two acres where he kept a cow and some chickens.

But that had ended when Timothy had changed from a *gut* and devoted son to someone Joshua didn't know. He argued about everything when he was talking, which wasn't often because he had days when he was sullen and did little more than grunt in response to anything Joshua or his siblings said.

"Go?" asked Samuel.

Joshua wasn't sure if the boy wanted to leave or wanted Joshua to leave, but Rebekah shook her head and took a cup out of a cupboard. The hinges screamed like a bobcat, and he saw her face flush.

"It needs some oil," he said quietly.

"I keep planning on doing that, but I get busy with other things, and it doesn't get done." She reached for the kettle and looked over her shoulder at him. "You know how it is."

"I know you must be overwhelmed here, but I'm

concerned more about the shape of your roof than a squeaky hinge. If Lloyd hadn't been able to maintain the farm on his own, he should have asked for help. We would have come right away."

"I know, but…"

When her eyes shifted, he let his sigh slip silently past his lips. She didn't want to talk about Lloyd, and he shouldn't push the issue. They couldn't change the past. He was well aware of how painful even thinking of his past with Matilda could be.

He thanked her when she set a cup of steeping tea in front of him. She went to the refrigerator, with her son holding her skirt, and came back with a small pitcher of cream. He hadn't expected her to remember he liked it in his tea.

"*Danki*, Rebekah." He gave her the best smile he could. "Now I'm the one saying it over and over."

"You don't need to say it for this." She set a piece of fresh apple pie in front of him. "I appreciate you having some of the pie. Otherwise I will eat most of it myself." She put her hand on her stomach, which strained the front of her dress. "It looks as if I've had enough."

"You are eating for two."

"As much as I've been eating, you'd think I was eating for a whole litter." She made a face as she pressed her hand to her side. "The way this *boppli* kicks, it feels like I'm carrying around a large crowd that is playing an enthusiastic game of volleyball."

He laughed and was rewarded with a brilliant smile from her. When was the last time he'd seen her genuine smile? He was sad to realize it'd been so long he didn't know.

After bringing a small cup of milk to the table, she

sat as he took one bite, then another of her delicious pie. Her son climbed onto her lap, and she offered him a drink. He drank but squirmed. Excusing herself, she stood and went into the other room with Samuel on her hip. She came back and sat. She put crayons and paper in front of her son, who began scribbling intently.

"This way he's occupied while we talk," she said.

"Gut." If he'd had any doubts about her love of *kinder*, they were gone now. She was a gentle and caring *mamm*.

"It's nice of you to come to visit, Joshua, but I know you, and you always have a reason for anything you do. Why are you here today?"

He should be thanking God for Rebekah giving him such a perfect opening to say for what he'd come to say. Yet words refused to form on his lips. Once he asked her to be his wife, there would be no turning back. He risked ruining their friendship, no matter how she replied. He hated the idea of jeopardizing that.

Samuel pushed a piece of paper toward him with a tentative smile.

"He wants you to have the picture he drew," Rebekah said.

Jacob looked at the crayon lines zigzagging across the page in every direction. "It's very colorful."

The little boy whispered in Rebekah's ear.

She nodded, then said, "He tells me it's a picture of your horse and buggy."

"I see," he replied, though he didn't. The collection of darting lines bore no resemblance he could discern to either Benny or his buggy. *"Gut* job, Samuel."

The *kind* started to smile, then hid his face in Rebekah's shoulder. She murmured something to him and picked up a green crayon. When she handed it to him along with another piece of paper, he began drawing again.

"You never answered my question, Joshua," she said. "Why did you come here today?"

"In part to apologize for not coming sooner. I should have been here to help you during the past few months."

Her smile wavered. "I know I've let the house and buildings go."

He started to ask another question, but when he met her steady gaze and saw how her chin trembled as she tried to hide her dismay, he nodded. "It doesn't take long once wind and rain get through one spot to start wrecking a whole building."

"That's true. I know I eventually will need to sell the farm. I've already had several offers to buy it."

"Amish or *Englisch*?"

"Both, though I wouldn't want to see the acres broken up and a bunch of *Englisch* houses built here."

"Some *Englischers* like to live on a small farm, as we do." He used the last piece of crust to collect the remaining apple filling on the plate. "My neighbors are like that."

"I didn't realize you had *Englisch* neighbors."

"Ja." He picked up his cup of tea. "Their Alexis and my Timothy have played together from the time they could walk."

"Will Alexis babysit for you?"

Joshua shook his head, lowering his untasted tea to the table. "She's involved in many activities at the high school and her part-time job, so she's seldom around. I hear her driving into their yard late every evening."

"Who's going to take care of Levi and Deborah while you're at work?"

God, You guided our conversation to this point. Be

with me now if it's Your will for this marriage to go forward.

He took a deep breath, then said, "I'm hoping you'll help me, Rebekah."

"Me? I'd be glad to once school is out, but come fall we live too far away for the *kinder* to walk here after school."

"I was hoping you might consider a move." He chided himself for what sounded like a stupid answer.

"I'd like to live in Paradise Springs, but I can't think of moving until I sell the farm. A lot needs to be repaired before I do, or I'll get next to nothing for it."

"I'd be glad to help."

"In exchange for babysitting?" She shook her head with a sad smile. "It's a *wunderbaar* idea, but it doesn't solve the distance problem."

He looked down at the table and the picture Samuel had drawn. Right now his life felt as jumbled as those lines. He couldn't meet Rebekah's eyes as he asked, "What if distance wasn't a problem?"

"I don't understand."

Talking in circles wasn't getting him anywhere and putting off asking the question any longer was *dumm*. He caught her puzzled gaze and held it, trying not to lose himself in her soft blue eyes. "Rebekah Burkholder, will you marry me?"

Rebekah choked on her gasp. She'd been puzzled about the reason for Joshua Stoltzfus's visit, but if she'd guessed every minute for the rest of her life, she couldn't have imagined it would be for him to propose.

Her son let out a protest, and she realized she'd tightened her hold around his waist until he couldn't breathe.

Loosening her arm, she set Sammy on the floor. She urged him to go and play with his wooden blocks stacked near the arch into the front room.

"He doesn't need to be a part of this conversation." She watched the little boy toddle to the blocks. She needed time to get her features back under control before she answered Joshua's astonishing question.

"I agree," Joshua said in a tense voice.

She clasped her hands in her lap and looked at him. His brown hair glistened in the sunlight coming through the kitchen windows, but his eyes, which were even darker, had become bottomless, shadowed pools. He was even more handsome than he'd been when she'd first met him years ago, because his sharply sculpted nose now fit with his other strong features. His black suspenders drew her eyes to his powerful shoulders and arms, which had been honed by years of building buggies. His broad hands, which now gripped the edge of the table, had been compassionate when they'd touched hers yesterday.

Had he planned to ask her to be his wife even then? Was that why he'd been solicitous of her and Sammy? She was confused because Joshua Stoltzfus didn't seem to have a duplicitous bone in his body. But if he hadn't been thinking about proposing yesterday, why had he today?

The only way to know was to ask. She forced out the words she must. "Why would you propose to me?"

"You need a husband, and I need a wife." His voice was as emotionless as if they spoke about last week's weather. "We've known each other for a very long time, and it's common for Amish widows and widowers to remarry. But even more important, you're Lloyd's widow."

"Why is that more important?"

"Lloyd and I once told each other that if something happened to one of us, we would take care of the other's family."

"It isn't our way to make vows."

"I know, but Lloyd was insistent that I agree to make sure his wife and family were cared for if something happened to him. I saw the *gut* sense and asked if he would do the same for me." He folded his arms on the table. "He was my friend, and I can't imagine anyone I would have trusted more with my family."

Rebekah quickly lowered her eyes from his sincere gaze. He truly believed Lloyd was the man she once had believed he was, too. She couldn't tell him the truth. Not about Lloyd, but she could tell him the truth about how foolish he was to ask her to be his wife.

"There's a big difference between taking care of your friend's family and…" She couldn't even say the word *marry*.

"But I haven't even taken care of you as I promised him."

"We've managed, and we will until I can sell the farm. *Danki* for your concern, Joshua. I appreciate what you are doing, but it's not necessary."

"I disagree. The fact remains I need a wife and you need a husband."

"You need a babysitter and I need a carpenter."

His lips twitched and she wanted to ask what he found amusing about this absurd conversation. Was it a jest he'd devised to make her smile? She pushed aside that thought as quickly as it'd formed. Joshua was a *gut* man. That was what everyone said, and she agreed. He wouldn't play such a prank on her. He must be sincere.

A dozen different emotions spiraled through her. She didn't know what to feel. Flattered that he'd considered her as a prospect to be his wife? Fear she might be as foolish as she had been the last time a man had proposed? Not that she believed Joshua would raise his hand and strike her, but then she hadn't guessed Lloyd would, either. And, to be honest, she never could have envisioned Joshua asking her to marry him.

"Rebekah," he said as his gaze captured hers again. "I know this is sudden, and I know you must think I'm *ab in kopp*—"

"The thought *you're crazy* has crossed my mind. More than once."

He chuckled, the sound soothing because it reminded her of the many other times she'd heard him laugh. He never laughed at another's expense.

"I'm sure it has, but I assure you that I haven't lost my mind." He paused, toyed with his cup, then asked, "Will you give me an answer, Rebekah? Will you marry me?"

"But why? I don't love you." Her cheeks turned to fire as she hurried to add, "That sounded awful. I'm sorry. The truth is you've always been a *gut* friend, Joshua, which is why I feel I can be blunt."

"If we can't speak honestly now, I can't imagine when we could."

"Then I will honestly say I don't understand why you'd ask me to m-m-marry you." She hated how she stumbled over the simple word.

No, it wasn't simple. There was nothing simple about Joshua Stoltzfus appearing at her door to ask her to become his wife. As he'd assured her, he wasn't *ab in kopp.* In fact, Joshua—up until today—had been the sanest man she'd ever met.

"Because we could help each other. Isn't that what a husband and wife are? Helpmeets?" He cleared his throat. "I would rather marry a woman I know and respect as a friend. We've both married once for love, and we've both lost the ones we love. Is it wrong to be more practical this time?"

Every inch of her wanted to shout, *"Ja!"* But his words made sense.

She had married Lloyd because she'd been infatuated with him and the idea of being his wife, so much so that she had convinced herself while they were courting to ignore how rough and demanding he had been with her when she'd caught the odor of beer on his breath. She'd accepted his excuses and his reassurances it wouldn't happen again...even when it had. She'd been blinded by love. How much better would it be to marry with her eyes wide open? No surprises and a husband whom she counted among her friends.

A pulse of excitement rushed up through her. She could escape, at last, from this farm, which had become a prison of pain and grief and second-guessing herself while she spun lies to protect the very person who had hurt her. She'd be a fool not to agree immediately.

Once she would have asked for time to pray about her decision, but she'd stopped reaching out to God when He hadn't delivered her from Lloyd's abuse. She believed in Him, and she trusted God to take care of the great issues of the world. Those kept Him so busy He didn't have time for small problems like hers.

"All right," she said. "I will marry you."

"Really?" He appeared shocked, as if he hadn't thought she'd agree quickly.

"Ja." She didn't add anything more, because there wasn't anything more to say. They would be wed, for better and for worse. And she was sure the worse couldn't be as bad as her marriage to Lloyd.

Chapter Three

Rebekah straightened her son's shirt. Even though Sammy was almost three, she continued to make his shirts with snaps at the bottom like a *boppli*'s gown. They kept his shirt from popping out the back of his pants and flapping behind him.

"It's time to go downstairs," she said to him as she glanced at her *mamm*, who sat on the bed in the room that once had been Rebekah and Lloyd's. "*Grossmammi* can't wait to have you sit with her."

"Sit with *Mamm*." His lower lip stuck out in a pout.

"But I have cookies." Almina Mast smiled at her grandson. She was a tiny woman, and her hair was the same white as her *kapp*. With a kind heart and a generous spirit, she and her husband Uriah had hoped for more *kinder*, but Rebekah had been their only one. The love they had heaped on her now was offered to Sammy.

"Cookies? *Ja, ja!*" He danced about to his tuneless song.

Mamm put a finger to her lips. "Quiet boys get cookies."

Sammy stilled, and Rebekah almost smiled at his antics. If she'd smiled, it would have been the first time since Joshua had asked her to marry three weeks ago. Since then the time had sped past like the landscape outside the window when she rode in an *Englischer*'s van last week while they'd gone to Lancaster to get their marriage license. Otherwise she hadn't seen him. She understood he was busy repairing equipment damaged during last year's harvest.

"Blessings on you, Rebekah." *Mamm* kissed her cheek. "May God bless you and bring you even more happiness with your second husband than he did with your first."

Rebekah stiffened. Did *Mamm* know the truth of how Lloyd had treated her? No, *Mamm* simply was wishing her a happy marriage.

A shiver ached along her stiff shoulders. Nobody knew what had happened in the house she'd shared with Lloyd. And she had no idea what life was like in Joshua Stoltzfus's home. His wife had always been cheerful when they'd been together, but so had Rebekah. Joshua showed affection for his wife and his *kinder*...as Lloyd had when he was sober.

She'd chosen the wrong man to marry once. What if she was making the same mistake? How well did she know Joshua Stoltzfus? At least she and Lloyd had courted for a while. She was walking into this marriage blind. Actually she was entering into it with her eyes wide open. She was familiar with the dark side of what Lloyd had called love. His true love had been for beer. She would watch closely and be prepared if Joshua began to drink. She would leave and return to her farm.

When *Mamm* left with Sammy, Rebekah kneaded her hands together. She was getting remarried. If tongues wagged because Lloyd hadn't been dead for a year, she hadn't heard it. She guessed most of the *Leit* here and in Paradise Springs thought she'd been smart to accept the proposal from a man willing to raise her two *kinder* along with his own.

The door opened again, and Leah Beiler and Joshua's sister Esther came in. They were serving as her attendants.

"What a lovely bride!" Leah gushed, and Rebekah wondered if Leah was thinking about when the day would come for her marriage to Joshua's younger brother Ezra. Leah was preparing to become a church member, and that was an important step toward marriage. Even though nothing had been announced and wouldn't be until the engagement was published two weeks before the marriage, it was generally suspected that the couple, who'd been separated for ten years, planned to wed in the fall.

Esther brushed invisible dust off the royal blue sleeve of Rebekah's dress. For this one day, Rebekah would be forgiven for not wearing black as she should for a year of mourning.

"Ja," Esther said as she moved to stand behind Rebekah. "It makes your eyes look an even prettier blue. Let us help you with your apron."

Every bride wore a white apron to match her *kapp* on her wedding day. She shouldn't have worn it again until she was buried with it, but Rebekah was putting it on for a second time today. Pulling it over her head, she slipped her arms through and let the sheer fabric settle on her dress.

"Oh." Esther chuckled. "There may be a problem."

Rebekah looked down and realized her wedding apron was stretched tightly across her belly. Looking over her shoulder at the other two women who were focused on the tabs that closed it with straight pins at the back, she asked, "Are they long enough?"

"I think so." Leah muttered something under her breath, then said, "There. They're pinned."

"Will it hold? It will be humiliating if one of the pins popped when I kneel."

"We'll pray they will stay in place." Esther chuckled. "If one goes flying, it'll make for a memorable wedding service."

Leah laughed, too. "I'm going to make my apron tabs extra long on my aprons from now on."

Rebekah couldn't manage more than a weak smile. "That's a *gut* idea."

The door opened and Joshua's daughter, Deborah, peeked in. "The ministers and the bishop have come in. Are you ready to go down?"

"Ja," Rebekah replied, though she wanted to climb out the window and run as far away as she could. What had she been thinking when she'd told Joshua yes? She was marrying a man whom she didn't love, a man who needed someone to watch his *kinder* and keep his house. She should have stopped this before it started. Now it was too late for second thoughts, but she was having second thoughts and third and fourth ones.

As she followed the others down the stairs to the room where the service was to be held, she tried not to think of the girl she'd been the last time she'd made this journey. It was impossible. She'd been optimistic and naive and in love as she'd walked on air to marry Lloyd Burkholder.

A longing to pray filled her, but she hadn't reached out to God in more than a year. She didn't know how to start now.

As she entered the room where more than two hundred guests stood, her gaze riveted on Joshua who waited among the men on the far side of the room. The sight of him dressed in his very best clothing and flanked by his two sons made the whole of this irrevocably real.

It has to be better than being married to Lloyd, she reminded herself. She and Sammy and her *boppli* wouldn't have to hide in an outbuilding as they had on nights when Lloyd had gone on a drunken rampage. She'd seen Joshua with his late wife, and he'd been an attentive husband. When Lloyd had teased him about doing a woman's work after Joshua brought extra lemonade out to the porch for them to enjoy, Joshua had laughed away his words.

But he doesn't love you. This is little more than a business arrangement.

She hoped none of her thoughts were visible as she affixed a smile in place and went with Leah and Esther to the bench facing the men's. As they sat so the service could begin, Sammy waved to her from where he perched next to *Mamm*. She smiled at him, a sincere smile this time. She was doing this for him. There was no price too high to give him a safe home.

Squaring her shoulders, she prepared herself to speak the words that would tie her life to Joshua Stoltzfus's for the rest of their lives.

Joshua put a hand on his younger son's shoulder. Levi always had a tough time sitting still, but the boy wiggled more every second as the long service went on. Usually Levi sat with the unmarried men and boys, where his squirming wasn't a problem. Maybe Joshua shouldn't have asked him to be one of his *Newehock-ers*, but Levi would have been hurt if Timothy had been asked and he hadn't.

He smiled his approval at Levi when the boy stopped shifting around on the bench. He meant to look at Reuben Lapp, their bishop who was preaching about the usual wedding service verses from the seventh chapter of the Book of Corinthians. His gaze went to Rebekah, who sat with her head slightly bowed.

Her red hair seemed to catch fire in the sunshine. A faint smile tipped the corners of her mouth, and he thought of how her eyes sparkled when she laughed. Were they bright with silver sparks now?

He'd almost forgotten how to breathe when he'd seen her walk into the room. This beautiful woman would be his wife. Even though tomorrow she would return to wearing black for the rest of her year of mourning for Lloyd, the rich blue of her dress beneath her white apron banished the darkness of her grief from her face. He felt blessed that she'd agreed to become his wife.

Joshua shook that thought out of his head. He was no lovesick young man who had won the heart of the girl he'd dreamed of marrying. Instead of letting his mind wander away on such thoughts, he should be listening to Reuben.

At the end of the sermon, the bishop said, "As we are gathered here to witness this marriage, it would seem there can't be any objections to it."

Beside Joshua, his oldest mumbled, "As if that would do any *gut*."

Joshua glanced at Timothy. His son hadn't voiced any protests about the marriage plans in the weeks since

Joshua had told his *kinder* Rebekah was to be his wife. Why now?

"Let the two who wish to marry come forward," Reuben said, saving Joshua from having to point out that Timothy could have raised his concerns earlier.

Or was his son taking the opportunity to be unpleasant, as he'd often been since he'd turned sixteen? Now was not the time to try to figure that out. Now was the time to do what was right for his *kinder* and Rebekah's while he fulfilled his promise to his best friend.

Joshua stood and watched as Rebekah did the same a bit more slowly. When he held out his hand to her, she took it. Relief rushed through him because he'd been unsure if she would. He should say something to her, but what? *Danki?* That wasn't what a bridegroom said to his future wife as they prepared to exchange vows.

He led her to Reuben, who smiled warmly at them. Joshua released Rebekah's hand and felt strangely alone. Of the more than two hundred people in the room, she was the only one who knew the truth of why they were getting married. He was glad they'd been honest with each other when he'd asked her to marry. Now there would be no misunderstandings between them, and they should be able to have a comfortable life.

Is that what you want? A comfortable life?

His conscience had been nagging him more as their wedding day drew closer. Every way he examined their arrangement, it seemed to be the best choice for them.

As long as you don't add love into the equation, or do you think you don't deserve love?

Ridiculous question. He'd had the love of his life with his first wife. No man should expect to have such a gift a second time.

"Is everything all right?" Reuben asked quietly.

Realizing the battle within him must have altered his expression, Joshua nodded. "Better than all right." He didn't look at Rebekah. If her face showed she was having second thoughts, too, he wasn't sure he could go through with the marriage. No matter how much they needed each other's help.

"*Gut.*" Raising his voice to be heard throughout the room, the bishop asked, "My brother, do you take our sister to be your wife until such hour as when death parts you? Do you believe this is the Lord's will, and your prayers and faith have brought you to each other?"

"*Ja.*"

Reuben looked at Rebekah and asked her the same, and Joshua felt her quiver. Or was he the one shaking? When she replied *ja*, he released the breath he'd been holding.

The bishop led them through their vows, and they promised to be loyal and stand beside each other no matter what challenges they faced. Rebekah's voice became steadier with each response. After Reuben placed her right hand in Joshua's right hand and blessed them, he declared them man and wife.

The simple words struck Joshua as hard as if a half-finished buggy had collapsed on him. Wife. Rebekah Burkholder was his wife. He was no longer a widower. He was a married man with four *kinder* and another on the way. The bonds that connected him to Matilda had been supplanted by the ones he had just made with Rebekah.

But I will love you always, Tildie.

He glanced guiltily at his new wife and saw her own face had grown so pale that her freckles stood out like chocolate chips in a cookie. Was she thinking the same thing about Lloyd?

It might not be an auspicious beginning for their marriage that their first thoughts after saying their vows were focused on the loves they had lost.

Rebekah stifled a yawn as the family buggy slowed to a stop in front of a simple house that was larger than the one she'd shared with Lloyd. The trip from Bird-in-Hand had taken almost a half hour, and Sammy had fallen asleep on her lap. He'd spent the day running around with the other youngsters. She had planned to have him sleep in his own bed tonight until Joshua asked her to return with him to his house. She'd hesitated, because a thunderstorm was brewing to the west. Even when he'd told her, with a wink, that it was his way of getting her away from the cleanup work at the end of their wedding day, she had hesitated. She'd agreed after *Mamm* had reminded her that a *gut* wife heeded her husband's wishes.

Joshua's three *kinder* sat behind them, and when she looked back she saw the two younger ones had fallen asleep, too. Timothy sat with his arms folded over his chest, and he was scowling. That seemed to be his favorite expression.

A flash caught her eye. Through the trees to the left glowed the bright lights she knew came from the house where the *Englischers* lived. She'd always had plain neighbors, and she hadn't thought about how the darkness at day's end would be disturbed by the glare of electric lights.

"The Grangers are *gut* neighbors," Joshua said as if she'd spoken her thoughts aloud. "That's their back porch light. They don't turn it on unless they're going to be out after dark, and they're considerate enough to turn it off when they get home. Brad put up a motion-detector light, but it kept lighting when an animal triggered it. Because it woke us, he went back to a regular light."

"They sound like nice people."

"Very. We have been blessed to have them as neighbors. Our *kinder* played together years ago, but now their older ones are off to college and only Alexis is at home."

"Are we going to sit here yakking all night?" asked Timothy. "It's stifling back here!"

Rebekah stiffened at his disrespectful tone, then she reminded herself they were tired.

Joshua jumped down before coming around to her side. "I'll carry him in." He held out his arms for Sammy.

She placed her precious *kind* in his arms, grateful for Joshua's thoughtfulness. She'd been on her feet too long today, and she'd become accustomed to taking a nap when Sammy did. As she stepped down, she didn't try to stifle her yawn.

"Let's get you inside," he said. "Then I'll take care of the horse."

"I'll put Benny away, *Daed*." Timothy bounced out and climbed on to the front seat after his brother and sister got out.

"*Danki*, but I expect you to come directly into the house when you're done."

"But, *Daed*, my friends—"

"Will see you on Saturday night as they always do."

Muttering something, Timothy drove the buggy toward the barn.

Joshua watched until the vehicle was swallowed by the building's shadow. Rebekah stood beside him, unsure if she should follow Deborah and Levi, who carried the bag she'd brought with a change of clothing for her and Sammy, into the house or remain by the man who was now her husband.

Husband! How long would it take her to get accustomed to the fact that she'd married Joshua? She was now Rebekah Mast Burkholder...Stoltzfus. Even connecting herself to him in her thoughts seemed impossible. She could have called a halt to the wedding plans right up until they'd exchanged vows. Reuben had given her that chance when he'd asked if everything was all right. Joshua had replied swiftly. Had he thought she might jilt him at the last minute?

"I'm sorry," Joshua said, jerking her away from her unsettling thoughts.

"For what?"

"I'd hoped Timothy would want to spend time with his family this one day at least." He looked down at Sammy. "He used to be as sweet as this little one."

Rebekah didn't know what to say. She started to put her hand on his arm to offer silent consolation. After pulling it back before she touched him, she locked her fingers in front of her. The easy camaraderie she'd felt for him was gone. Everything, even ordinary contact between friends, had changed with a few words. Nothing was casual any longer. Any word, any motion, any glance had taken on a deeper meaning.

Feeling as if she'd already disappointed him because she had said nothing, she followed him into the light green kitchen. Joshua turned on the propane floor lamp while Levi lit a kerosene lantern in the center of the table.

Again Rebekah was speechless, but this time with shock. Every flat surface, including the stove and the top of the refrigerator, was covered with stacks of dirty dishes. What looked to be a laundry basket was so full that the clothes had fallen into jumbled heaps around it. She couldn't tell if the clothes were clean or dirty.

"*Daedi* cooked our breakfast," Deborah said in a loud whisper beneath the hiss of the propane.

Joshua had the decency to look embarrassed as he set Sammy on the floor. Her son had woken as they'd stepped inside. "I meant to clean the house before you arrived, Rebekah, but I had a rush job yesterday, and then we had to get over to your house early today and…" He leaned one hand on the table, then yanked it away with a grimace.

Going to the sink beneath a large window, Rebekah dampened a dishrag. She took it to Joshua and as he wiped his hand off said, "You asked me to come back here tonight because you didn't want me to have to straighten up at my house after such a long day. And then you brought me *here* to *this*?" She burst into laughter. Maybe it was fueled by exhaustion and the stress of pretending to be a happy bride. The whole situation was so ludicrous that if she didn't laugh, she'd start weeping.

"I can see where you'd find that confusing," he said as he glanced around the kitchen.

"Confusing?" More laughter erupted from her, and she pressed her hands over her belly. "Is that what you call this chaos?"

Deborah giggled. "*Daedi* always uses twice as many dishes and pans because he starts making one thing and ends up cooking something else entirely."

"It's usually because I don't have one of the ingredients," Joshua said, his lips twitching.

"Or you don't remember the recipe," Levi crowed.

"*Ja*, that's true." Joshua dropped the dishrag on the table and took off his best hat. "I can put a buggy together with my eyes closed—or near to that—but baking a casserole trips me up every time."

Laughter filled the kitchen as everyone joined in.

Picking up the cloth, Rebekah put it on the sink. "I'll face this in the morning."

"A *gut* idea." To his *kinder*, he said, "Off to bed with you."

"Will you come up for our prayers?" Levi asked.

"*Ja.*"

Deborah took Sammy's hand. "*Komm* upstairs with me."

"No," Rebekah and Joshua said at the same time.

The little girl halted, clearly wondering what she'd done wrong.

"I'll put him to bed," Rebekah added. "Everything is new to him. Sammy, why don't you give Deborah and Levi hugs?"

The little boy, who was half asleep on his feet, nodded and complied.

"You're my brother now." Deborah's smile brightened her whole face. "When we found out *Daedi* was going to marry you, Rebekah, I was happy. I'm not the *boppli* of the family any longer."

"Sammy will be glad to have a big sister and big brothers." She looked at Levi, who gave her a shy smile. Should she offer to hug the *kinder*, too?

Before she could decide, the back door opened. Timothy came in, bringing a puff of humid air with him. He glared at them, especially Joshua, before striding through the kitchen. His footsteps resounded on the stairs as he went up.

Rebekah saw Joshua's eyes narrow. Timothy hadn't spoken to her once. At sixteen he didn't need a *mamm*, but perhaps he would come to see her as someone she could trust. Maybe even eventually as a friend.

Subdued, Deborah and Levi went out of the kitchen. Their footfalls were much softer on the stairs.

"I'm sorry," Joshua said into the silence.

She scooped up Sammy and cradled him. "He's a teenager. It's not easy."

"I realize that, but I hope you realize his rudeness isn't aimed at you. It's aimed at me." He rubbed his hand along his jaw, then down his beard. "I don't know how to handle him because I wasn't a rebellious kid myself."

"I wasn't, either."

"Too bad." The twinkle returned to his eyes. "If you'd been, you might be able to give me some hints on dealing with him."

She smiled at his teasing. He'd been someone she'd deemed a friend for years. She must—they must—make sure they didn't lose that friendship as they navigated this strange path they'd promised to walk together.

Joshua pointed at her and put a finger to his lips. She looked down to see Sammy was once more asleep. Joshua motioned for her to come with him.

Rebekah followed him through the living room. It looked as it had the last time she had been there before Matilda died. The same furniture, the same paint, the same sewing machine in a corner. She glanced toward the front door. The same wooden clock that didn't work. With a start she realized that under the piles of dishes and scattered clothing the kitchen was identical to when

Matilda had been alive. It was as if time had stopped in this house with Matilda's last breath.

Opening a door on the other side of the stairs, Joshua lit a lamp. The double bed was topped by a wild-goose-chase-patterned quilt done in cheerful shades of red and yellow and blue. He walked past it to a small bed his *kinder* must have used when they were Sammy's age. Another pretty quilt, this one in the sunshine-and-shadow pattern done in blacks and grays and white, was spread across it. Drawing it back along with the sheet beneath it, he stepped aside so she could slip the little boy in without waking him.

She straightened and looked around. The bedroom was large. A tall bureau was set against the wall opposite the room's two windows, and the bare floors shone with years of care. A quartet of pegs held a *kapp*, a dusty black bonnet and a straw hat. She wasn't surprised when Joshua placed his *gut* hat on the empty peg.

This must have been Joshua and Matilda's room. Suddenly the room seemed way too small. Aware of Joshua going to the bureau and opening the drawers, she lowered the dark green shades on the windows. She doubted Sammy would sleep late in the morning. Usually he was up with the sun.

She faced Joshua and saw he had gathered his work clothes. He picked them up from the blanket chest at the foot of the bed. His gaze slowly moved along her, and so many emotions flooded his eyes she wasn't sure if he felt one or all at the same time. Realizing she was wringing her hands, she forced her arms to her sides.

It was the first time they'd been alone as man and wife. They stood in the room he'd shared with his first wife. She didn't trust her voice to speak, even if she had the slightest idea what to say as she looked at the man who was now her husband. The weight on the first word she spoke was enormous. There were a lot of things she wanted to ask about the life they'd be sharing. She didn't know how.

"Gut nacht," he said into the strained silence. "I'll be upstairs. Second door to the left. Don't hesitate to knock if you or Samuel need anything. I know it'll take you a while to get used to living in a new place."

"Dunki."

He waited, but she couldn't force her lips to form another word. Finally, with a nod, he began to edge past her. When she jumped back, fearful he was angry with her, he stared at her in astonishment.

"Are you okay?" he asked.

She nodded, though she was as far from okay as she could be. It was beginning again. The ever-present anxiety of saying or doing the wrong thing and being punished by her husband's heavy hand.

"Are you sure?" His eyes searched her face, so she struggled to keep her expression calm as she nodded again.

He started to say something else, then seemed to think better of it. He bid her *gut nacht* again before he went out of the room.

She pressed her hands to her mouth to silence her soft sob as the tears she'd kept dammed for the whole day cascaded down her cheeks. She should be grateful Joshua had given her and Sammy this lovely room. And she was. But she also felt utterly alone and scared.

"What have I done?" she whispered to the silence.

She'd made, she feared, another huge mistake by doing the wrong thing for the right reasons.

Chapter Four

Joshua's first thought when he opened his eyes the next morning was, *Where am I?* The angle of the ceiling was wrong. There was a single window, and the walls were too close to the bed.

Memory rushed through his mind like a tempest, wild and flowing in every direction. Yesterday he'd married Rebekah, his best friend's widow.

Throwing back the covers, he put his feet on the rug by the bed. His beloved Tildie had started making rugs for the bedrooms shortly after they were wed, and she'd replaced each one when it became too worn. As he looked down through the thick twilight before dawn, he saw rough edges on the one under his feet. Sorrow clutched his heart. His sweet wife would never make another rug for the *kinder*.

Rebekah was his wife now. For better or for worse, and for as long as they lived.

He drew in a deep breath, then let it sift past his taut lips. He'd honored Lloyd's request, and he shouldn't have any regrets. He didn't. Just a question.

Where did he and Rebekah go from here?

Unable to answer that, because he was not ready to consider the question too closely, he pushed himself to his feet. He dressed and did his best to shave his upper lip without a mirror. As he pulled his black suspenders over his shoulders, he walked out of the bedroom.

Light trickled from beneath one door on the other side of the hall. He heard heavy footfalls beyond it. Timothy must already have gotten up, which was a surprise because most mornings Joshua had to wake his older son. Not hearing any voices, he guessed Levi was still asleep. Not even the cacophony of a thunderstorm could wake the boy. The other doorway was dark. He considered making sure Deborah was up so she wouldn't be late for school, but decided to let her sleep. It had been late by the time the *kinder* had gone to bed last night.

As he went down the stairs, Joshua heard the rumble of a car engine and the crunch of tires on gravel. His neighbor must be heading into Philadelphia this morning. Brad always left before sunup when he wanted to catch the train into the city, because he had to drive a half hour east to reach the station.

It was the only normal thing today, because as he reached the bottom of the stairs, he smelled the enticing aromas of breakfast cooking. He glanced at the bedroom where he usually slept. The door was closed.

The propane lamp hissed in the kitchen as he walked in to see Rebekah at the stove. She wore a dark bandana over her glistening hair. Beneath her simple black dress and apron, her feet were bare.

"Sit down," she said as if she'd made breakfast for him dozens of times. "Do you want milk in your *kaffi*?"

"No, I drink it black in the morning."

"Are the others awake?"

"Only Timothy." He was astounded how they spoke about such ordinary matters. There was nothing ordinary about Rebekah being in his kitchen before dawn.

"*Gut.* I assumed he'd get up early, too, so I made plenty of eggs and bacon." Turning from the stove, she picked up a plate topped by biscuits. She took a single step toward the table, then halted as her gaze locked with his.

A whirlwind of emotions crisscrossed her face, and he knew he should say something to put her at ease. But what? Her fingers trembled on the plate. Before she could drop it, he reached for it. His knuckle brushed hers so lightly he wouldn't have noticed the contact with anyone else. A heated shiver rippled across his hand and up his arm. He tightened his hold on the plate before *he* let it fall to the floor.

He put the biscuits on the table as she went back to the stove. Searching for something to say, he had no chance before Timothy entered the kitchen. His son walked to the table, his head down, not looking either right or left as he took his seat to the left of Joshua's chair at the head of the table.

Rebekah came back. Setting the coffeepot on a trivet in the center of the table, she hesitated.

"Why don't you sit here?" Joshua asked when he realized she was unsure which chair to use. He pointed to the one separated from his by the high chair he'd brought down from the attic before the wedding yesterday. He'd guessed she would want it for her son, but now discovered it created a no-man's-land between them.

She nodded as she sat. Was that relief he saw on her face? Relief they were no longer alone in the kitchen?

Relief the high chair erased any chance their elbows might inadvertently bump while they ate?

He pushed those thoughts aside as he bent his head to signal it was time for the silent grace before they ate. His prayers were more focused on his new marriage than food, and he hoped God wouldn't mind. After all, God knew the truth about why he'd asked Rebekah to be his wife.

As soon as Joshua cleared his throat to end the prayer, Timothy reached for the bowl containing fluffy eggs. He served himself, then passed the bowl to Joshua. That was followed by biscuits and apple butter as well as bacon and sausage.

Each bite he took was more delicious. The biscuits were so light he wondered why they hadn't floated up from the plate while they'd prayed. The *kaffi* had exactly the right bite for breakfast. He could not recall the last time he'd enjoyed a second cup at breakfast, because his own brew resembled sludge.

For the first time in months, Timothy was talkative. He had seconds and then thirds while chattering about a baseball game he'd heard about yesterday at the wedding, a game won by his beloved Phillies. It was as if the younger version of his son had returned, banishing the sulky teen he'd become. Even after they finished their breakfast with another silent prayer, Timothy was smiling as he left to do the barn chores he usually complained should be Levi's now that he worked every day at the buggy shop.

Joshua waited until the back door closed behind his oldest, then said, "Tell me how you did that."

"Did what?" Rebekah asked as she rose and picked up the used plates. After setting them on top of others stacked on the counter, she began running water to begin the massive task of washing the dirty dishes that had gathered since the last time he'd helped Deborah with them.

"Make my oldest act like a human being rather than a grumpy mule," he replied.

"Don't let him—or any of the other *kinder*—hear you say that. He wouldn't appreciate it."

"Or having his sister and brother repeat it."

"And Sammy, too. *Kinder* his age grab on to a word and use it over and over." She smiled as she put soap into the water and reached for a dishrag. Not finding one, she glanced around.

"Second drawer," he said, hoping there was a clean dishcloth. Like the dishes, laundry had piled up, ignored during the past week.

"Danki." She opened the drawer and pulled out a cloth. "I'll get accustomed to where everything is eventually."

He knew she didn't mean to, but her words were like a pail of icy water splashing in his face. A reminder that no matter how much they might pretend, everything had changed.

No, not everything. He still held on to his love for Tildie.

That will never change, he silently promised his late wife.

Never, because he wasn't going to chance putting his heart through such pain ever again.

Everything seemed unfamiliar in the Stoltzfus kitchen, yet familiar at the same time.

Rebekah was cooking breakfast as she did each

morning while she waited for the bread dough to rise a second time. She prepared enough for Levi and Deborah. Or she thought she had until she saw Levi could tuck away as much as his older brother. She fried the last two eggs for the boy, who ate them with enthusiasm.

"You cook *gut*! Real *gut*!" Levi said as he took his straw hat off the peg by the back door. With a grin at his sister, he added, "You should learn from her."

"She will," Rebekah replied gently when she saw the dismay on the little girl's face. "After school, Levi, while you are doing your chores, Deborah and I will be preparing your supper."

She was rewarded by a broad smile from Joshua's daughter, who said, "Levi is going to *Onkel* Daniel's shop after school." Deborah picked up the blue plastic lunch box and stepped aside so her brother could take the green one. "I'll be walking home with Mandy Beiler. Mandy lives down the road from *Grossmammi* Stoltzfus. She used to live in Philadelphia, but she lives here now. She is almost the same age I am. We—"

"We need to go." Levi frowned at his sister. "We don't want to arrive after the school bell rings. We won't have time to play baseball if we're late."

Deborah rolled her eyes as if ancient and world-weary. "All he thinks about is baseball."

"Like Timothy," Rebekah said as she wiped Sammy's hands before giving him another half biscuit.

"Timothy thinks about girls, too, especially Alexis next door. He talks to her every chance he can get." Levi put his hand over his mouth and gave a guilty glance toward his sister.

"I'm sure he does," Rebekah said quietly. "They've been friends their whole lives, haven't they?"

"*Ja*, friends." Deborah scowled at her brother. "Saying otherwise is silly. She is *Englisch*."

Levi nodded and opened the door. His smile returned when he added, "At the wedding he was talking to some girls from Bird-in-Hand. I think he really liked—"

"Whom he likes is Timothy's business." Rebekah smiled. "You know we don't talk about such things, so it can be a surprise when a couple is published to marry."

"Like you and *Daedi*?" asked Deborah. "Lots of folks were surprised. I heard them say so."

Nobody more than I, she was tempted to reply, but she made a shooing motion toward the door. The two scholars skipped across the yard to where their scooters were waiting. They hooked their lunch boxes over the handles before pushing them along the driveway toward the road.

She prayed the Lord would keep them safe. There were fewer cars along this road than in Bird-in-Hand, where carloads of tourists visited shops and restaurants.

She remained in the doorway and looked at the gray clouds thickening overhead. She hadn't expected to watch *kinder* leave for school for another couple of years. When Deborah looked over her shoulder and waved, the tension that had kept Rebekah tossing and turning last night diminished.

Help me make this marriage work, Lord, she prayed. *For the* kinder*'s sakes. They have known too much sorrow, and it's time for them to be happy as* kinder *should be.*

Seeing Sammy had found the box of crayons she'd packed to bring to Joshua's house, Rebekah turned to the sink. She had to refill the sink with the water heated by solar panels on the roof. When she'd met Joshua's second-youngest brother, Micah, at the wedding, he'd mentioned how he had recently finished the installation.

She hummed a tuneless song as she washed dishes, dried them and put them in the cupboards. Outside, it began to rain steadily. Maybe she should have told the *kinder* to take umbrellas to school.

By the time she had baked the bread as well as a batch of snickerdoodles, it was time for the midday meal. Lloyd always wanted his big meal at noon, but Joshua worked off the farm, so she would prepare their dinner for the evening. She had no idea what Joshua and his *kinder* liked to eat.

Rebekah pushed aside that thought as she put Sammy in the high chair and gave him his sandwich and a glass of milk. Sitting beside him, she ate quickly, then returned to work. She was scooping up an armful of dirty laundry from the floor when she heard Sammy call her.

Turning, she asked over her shoulder, "What is it, *liebling*?"

"Go home?" Thick tears rolled down his full cheeks.

She dropped the clothes to the floor. Sitting, she lifted Sammy out of the high chair and set him beside her. There wasn't enough room on her lap for him any longer. Putting her arm around his shoulders, she nestled him close. Her heart ached to hear his grief.

"I thought we would stay here and see Deborah and Levi when they get home from school," she said and kissed the top of his head.

"When that?"

"After Sammy has his nap."

He wiggled away and got down. "Nap now?"

"Not until you finish your sandwich." As she set him back in the high chair, she smiled at how eager he was to see Joshua's younger *kinder* again.

In Bird-in-Hand, Sammy had encountered other *kinder* only on church Sundays. Their neighbors didn't have youngsters, and even if they had, Sammy was too young to cross the fields on his own. She'd become accustomed to remaining home in the months before Lloyd's death because he had flown into rages when he didn't know where she was. After his death, she'd had an excuse to stay behind her closed door.

But it hadn't been fair to Sammy.

Guilt clamped around her heart. Now *that* was familiar. Each time Lloyd had lashed out at her, she'd tried to figure out what she'd done to make him strike her again.

She was Joshua Stoltzfus's wife now. Her past was gone, buried with Lloyd.

Repeating it over and over to convince herself, she cleaned Sammy up after his lunch. She took him into the bedroom for his nap, but he was too excited. Each time she settled him on the small bed with his beloved stuffed dog, he was up afterward and sneaking out of the bedroom to explore the house.

Rebekah gave up after a half hour. Skipping his nap one day wouldn't hurt him, and she was curious, too, about the rest of the house. She glanced around the kitchen. The dishes were cleaned and put away, though she suspected she hadn't put them in their proper places. She would check with Deborah so everything was as it should be when Joshua arrived home. The dirty clothes were piled on the floor in the laundry room. In the morning before breakfast, if the rain stopped, she would start the first load. She hadn't mopped the floor. That made no sense when Joshua and the *kinder* would be tracking in water and mud.

There wasn't any reason for her *not* to explore the house.

Sammy grinned and chattered like an excited squirrel as they walked into the large front room where church could be held when it was their turn to host it. She wondered when that would be. Surely no one would expect the newlyweds to hold church at their house right away. Most newlyweds spent the first month of their marriage visiting family and friends nearby and far away. Joshua hadn't mentioned making calls, and she guessed his business wouldn't allow him time away. Just as well, because she didn't want to upset Sammy by uprooting him day after day.

When her son scrambled up the stairs, dragging the stuffed dog with him, she followed slowly, not wanting to slip on the smooth, wooden steps. But there was another reason she hesitated. She hoped Joshua wouldn't care if she went upstairs while he was at the buggy shop. Last night he'd told her to come and get him if she or Sammy needed anything, so her exploring shouldn't make him angry.

She wrapped her arms around herself. She hated how every thought, every action, had to be considered with care. After Lloyd's death, she'd been gloriously free from a husband's expectations. Now she was subjected to them once more. But would Joshua be as heavy-handed as Lloyd had been? She must make sure she never found out.

Lord, is this Your will? If so, guide my steps and my words on a path where we will remain safe.

Rebekah opened the first door on the second floor. A pair of dresses hung from pegs on the wall, along with a white apron Deborah would wear to church. A black bonnet waited beside them. By the window, the bed was covered with a beautiful quilt. The diamond-in-a-square pattern was done in cheerful shades of blue, purple and green. A rag rug beside the bed would keep little feet from the chill of a wintry floor.

The room beside it clearly belonged to Timothy because a man-size pair of shoes were set beneath the window, but a second mattress had been dragged into the room. She realized Levi must have given up his room to Joshua and was sleeping with his brother. She appreciated the boys' kindness, especially when they had no idea how long Levi would be sharing with Timothy.

Sammy ran to the door across the hall. She hurried after him, not wanting him to disturb Joshua's things. Grabbing her son's arm, she remained in the doorway.

Nothing about the room gave her a clue to the man she'd married. It was the same as the other rooms, except the ceiling slanted sharply on either side of a single dormer. Like his *kinder*'s rooms, the bed was neatly made and a rag rug brightened the wooden floor. She hadn't realized how she'd hoped to find something to reassure her that he was truly as gentle as he appeared. If he proved to be a chameleon like Lloyd...

"Cold, *Mammi*?" asked Sammy.

She smiled at him, even as she curbed another shiver. If a *kind* as young as her son could sense her disquiet, she must hide her feelings more deeply. She could not allow Joshua to suspect the secrets of her first marriage.

If the truth of Lloyd's weaknesses became known, it could ruin her son's life.

She wouldn't let that happen.

Ever.

Chapter Five

As he drove toward his house, Joshua couldn't recall another day at the buggy shop that had seemed so long. Usually the hours sped past as he kept himself occupied with the work and trying to teach Timothy the skills his son would need to take over the shop after him.

He *had* been busy today, but his thoughts hadn't stayed on the antique carriage he was restoring for Mr. Carpenter, an *Englischer* who lived in a fancy community north of Philadelphia. Too often instead of the red velvet he was using to reupholster the interior of the vehicle that dwarfed his family buggy, Joshua had seen Rebekah's face.

Her uncertainty when she'd stood beside him in front of their bishop to take their wedding vows. Her laughter when they'd come into the messy kitchen. Her glowing eyes filled with questions as he bid her *gut nacht*. Her kind smile for his teenage son this morning.

"Watch out!" Timothy shouted as Levi yelped a wordless warning from behind him.

Joshua yanked on the reins, though the horse had already started to turn away from the oncoming milk truck. The driver gave a friendly wave as the vehicle rumbled past before turning into the lane leading to a neighboring farm.

Lowering his hands to his lap, Joshua took a steadying breath. He couldn't get so lost in his thoughts that he missed what was going on around him. He'd lost Tildie. He couldn't bear the idea of losing his two sons.

Help me focus, Lord, on what is important in my life.

"Want me to drive, *Daed*?" asked Timothy with a grin.

"I'll drive!" Levi wasn't going to be left out, especially after assisting his *onkel* at Daniel's carpentry shop.

"*Danki*, but I think I can manage to get us home from here in one piece." Joshua kept his eyes on the road as he guided the horse onto the driveway. He sent up a prayer of gratitude that he and his two sons hadn't been hurt.

What was wrong with him? He was showing less sense than his teenage son. If Timothy had been driving, Joshua would have reprimanded him for not paying attention. Even after he'd brought the buggy to a stop between the house and the barn, his hands shook. He nodded when Levi offered to help Timothy unhook Benny and get the horse settled for the night.

"Dinner will be on the table soon," he said as he did every evening after work. "So don't dawdle."

"Are you sure your bride will have it ready?" Timothy asked.

He glanced at his grinning teenage son. Tempted to remind his son that Timothy didn't know anything about Rebekah, he refrained. Joshua would have to admit he didn't know much about her, either. He wasn't going to confess that to his *kinder*.

"We'll see, won't we?" Joshua strode toward the kitchen door.

He paused to check the garden. It needed weeding again. He glanced at the chicken coop. The patch he'd put on the roof last month was still in *gut* shape. Reaching up, he gave the clothesline that ran from the back stoop to the barn a gentle tug. The tension remained *gut*, so he didn't need to tighten it yet to keep clean clothes from dragging in the grass.

Joshua sighed. He'd told the boys not to dawdle, and he was doing it himself. *Coward!* When he'd asked Rebekah to wed him, he'd known there would be changes. There had to be, because the marriage was bringing her and a toddler and soon a *boppli* into the family. He'd convinced himself he understood that.

But he hadn't.

Not really.

Knowing he could not loiter in his own yard any longer, he climbed the two steps to the small porch at the back door. He wasn't sure what he'd find, but when he opened the back door, he stared. Every inch of the kitchen shone like a pond in the bright sunlight. Even the stain he'd assumed would never come out of the counter was gone. Dishes were stacked neatly in the cupboards, and each breath he drew in contained the luscious aromas of freshly baked bread as well as the casserole Rebekah was removing from the oven.

The last time the kitchen had smelled so enticing was before Tildie became ill. Supper at his *mamm*'s house was accompanied by great scents, but his own kitchen had been filled with odors of smoke and scorched pans and foods that didn't go together.

His gaze riveted on her. Strands of red hair had escaped her *kapp* and floated around her face like wisps of cloud. Her face glowed with the heat from the oven, and she smiled as she drew in a deep breath of the steam coming from the casserole.

He had never seen her look so beautiful or so at ease. The thought shocked him. He'd always considered her pretty, but he'd never thought about how taut her shoulders usually were. Not just since he'd asked her to marry. Every time he'd seen her.

"Daedi!"

Deborah rushed over and threw her arms around his waist. He embraced her, turning his attention from Rebekah and the kitchen's transformation to his daughter. Her smile was wider than he'd seen in a long time. She must have enjoyed her time with Rebekah and Sammy after school.

A pulse of an unexpected envy tugged at him. He dismissed it, not wanting to examine too closely how he wished he could have shared that time with them.

"Perfect timing," Rebekah said as she carried the casserole of scalloped potatoes to the table. Platters of sliced roast beef were set beside bowls holding corn and green beans. Sliced bread was flanked by butter and apple butter. Chowchow and pickled beets completed the feast. She looked past him, and he realized Timothy and Levi stood behind him when she asked, "Do you boys need to wash up?"

His mouth watered. His sons' expressions were bright with anticipation, and he wondered if his own face looked the same. Even so, he motioned for the boys to go into the laundry room to wash their hands. They went with a speed he hadn't seen them show before dinner…ever.

As he went to the kitchen sink, he almost bumped into Sammy, who was racing to his *mamm*. The *kind* glanced at him fearfully. He hoped the little boy would get used to him soon. Maybe in his own young way Sammy mourned for Lloyd and wasn't ready to replace his *daed* with another man.

Joshua doubted he could ever be the man Lloyd Burkholder had been. When people spoke of Lloyd, they always mentioned his dedication to his neighbors and his family. More than once, he'd heard someone say Lloyd always accompanied Rebekah wherever she went. A truly devoted husband. With his work taking him to the shop each day, Joshua couldn't be the doting husband his friend had been. He hoped Rebekah understood.

As soon as everyone was seated at the table, he signaled for them to bow their heads for silent grace. He was pleased to see Sammy do so, too. Rebekah had taught her son well.

He didn't linger over his prayers, which again had more to do with making his new marriage work and less to do with the food in front of him. Clearing his throat, he raised his head. The *kinder* didn't need prompting to start passing the food along the table.

His worry about what to discuss during the meal vanished when Levi monopolized the conversation. His younger son was excited that he'd learned how to use one of the specialty saws Daniel had for his construction projects. As he described the tool in detail, Rebekah helped Sammy eat with as little mess as possible. Deborah and Timothy were busy enjoying the meal.

Joshua realized he was, too. He'd been dependent on his own cooking or Deborah's struggling attempts for too long. There had been plenty of meals at his *mamm*'s house, but even she wasn't the cook Rebekah was. Each dish he tried was more flavorful than the one before. Like his sons, he had seconds.

"Don't fill up completely," Rebekah said as she smiled at his daughter. "There's peach pie for dessert."

"You're spoiling us with your *wunderbaar* food," he replied.

She flushed prettily when the boys hurried to add their approval. She deflected it by saying quietly, "God gave each of us a unique talent, and the praise should go to Him."

Deborah jumped up, announcing she would serve dessert. She cut the pie and brought the first plate to the table and set it in front of Joshua with a hopeful smile. "Try it, *Daedi*." Her voice dropped almost to a whisper. "I made it."

"You made the pie, Deborah?" He hoped his disappointment didn't come through in his voice. As *gut* as the rest of the meal had been, he'd been looking forward to sampling Rebekah's peach pie. She'd brought one to the house years ago, and he still recalled how delicious it had been.

Her brothers regarded the pieces their sister handed them with suspicion. As one they glanced at him. Neither reached for a fork, even when Deborah sat again at the table. When dismay lengthened his daughter's face, he couldn't delay any longer.

Picking up his fork, he broke off a corner from the pie. Flakes fell on to the plate. That was a surprise because Deborah's last attempt at making a pie had resulted in a crust as crisp as a cracker. Aware how everyone was watching, he raised the fork to his mouth.

Flavors came to life on his tongue. Peaches, cinnamon and even a hint of nutmeg.

"This is..." He had to search for the best word. Not *surprising* or *astounding* and most especially not *impossible*, though he couldn't believe Deborah had made the flaky crust that was as light as the biscuits at breakfast. When his daughter regarded him with anticipation, he finished, "Beyond *wunderbaar*."

"Danki," his daughter said as she turned toward the other end of the table to watch her brothers dig in now that Joshua had announced the pie was *gut*. "Rebekah taught me a really easy way to make the crust. It's important not to handle it too much. Mix it, roll it out and get it in the pan."

"She did a *gut* job." He broadened his smile as he took another bite.

"It wasn't hard when I have such an eager student," Rebekah replied,

When they finished the meal with a silent prayer, Joshua asked Timothy to help Levi with the dishes while Deborah played with Sammy. Before they could answer, he stood and invited Rebekah to come out on the front porch with him. He wasn't sure who looked the most surprised at his requests.

But one thing he knew for certain. He and Rebekah needed some time to talk and come to terms with the life they had chosen together. He had put off the discussion since he asked her to be his wife.

Rebekah lifted Sammy down from the high chair and told him to show Deborah the pictures he'd colored earlier. As the toddler rushed to the little girl, he shot an uneasy glance in Joshua's direction. His *mamm* looked dismayed, and she bit her lower lip.

Joshua said nothing as he motioned for her to lead the way to the front door. When he reached over her head to hold the screen door, she recoiled sharply. Had he surprised her? She must have known he was right behind her, and she should have guessed he'd hold the door for her.

A grim realization rushed through him. She must be worried that if she lowered the walls between them, even enough to thank him for a common courtesy, he would insist on his rights as her husband. He wanted to reassure her that he understood her anxiety, but anything he could think to say might make the situation even more tense.

If that were even possible.

Scolding herself for showing her reaction to Joshua's hand moving past her face, Rebekah knew she needed to take care. He hadn't been about to slap her, and acting as if he was could betray the secret she kept in the darkest corners of her heart. She hurried to the closer of the two rocking chairs on the front porch. She'd always loved the rockers Joshua and Matilda had received as wedding gifts. Whenever she and Lloyd had visited, she had happily sat in one and watched the traffic on the narrow road in front of the house.

Now...

She pushed aside thoughts of being a trespasser. Upon marrying Joshua, this had become her home. She had to stop considering it another woman's.

"I thought you might appreciate a bit of rest," Joshua said as he leaned against the railing so he could face her. "I never expected you to toil so hard in the kitchen."

"You know how it is. You do one thing and that leads

to another and then to another, and before you know it, the whole task is done."

He smiled and something spun with joy within her. He was a handsome man, even more so when he grinned because his dark brown eyes glistened. He was past due for a haircut, and strands fell forward into his eyes. She folded her hands on her lap to keep from reaching up to discover if it was as silken as it looked.

"And I had lots of help," she added so silence didn't fall between them. "Deborah is like a sponge, soaking up everything I tell her."

"Especially about making pie." He patted his stomach. "I may have to take up jogging like the *Englischers* if you keep feeding us such amazing food."

"If you do, I will sew an under-the-chin strap for your hat like I do for Sammy's so it won't bounce off."

He roared a laugh, slapping his hand against the roof pole beside him. She smiled, glad she'd been able to ease the strain on his face…if only for a short time.

When he waved at a buggy driving past, he said, "Daniel is late returning home tonight. I wonder if he is courting someone again."

"Sometimes it takes time to find the right person to marry."

"Oh, that doesn't seem to be his problem." He stared after the buggy until it vanished over a hill. "I hope this time he doesn't get cold feet and put an end to it. He's courted two different girls we thought he might wed. The girls joined the church in anticipation of a proposal, but he hasn't been baptized. They married other men."

"Maybe he isn't ready."

"I was baptized, married and had a *kind* by the time I was his age."

She slowed her rocking to stop. "Each of us is different, Joshua. Daniel will make the right decision when it's God's will for him to do so."

"*Ja*. Daniel is a *gut* man." With a sigh he looked back at her. "I meant to ask you. Daniel was glad to have Levi help him this afternoon. He'd like Levi to come back a day or two each week if you can spare him."

"It would be *gut* for Levi to learn more about what his *onkel* does." She smiled as she began rocking again slowly and watched the lights from a car ripple through the trees along the road. "With only a few years of school left for him, he can learn about a craft he might want to pursue."

"My thoughts exactly, but I don't want him neglecting his chores here. The garden needs—"

"Deborah, Sammy and I will take care of the garden. You don't need to worry about it."

"I wasn't." He paused and looked everywhere but at her. "How did Sammy do today?"

"He spent the day exploring the house. Fortunately I was able to block the cellar door with a chair before he took it into his head to investigate down there."

Again he drew in a deep breath. "I know it may take time, but I wish he felt more comfortable around me."

"It *will* take time."

"I know that, but I wish he wouldn't cringe away in fear. Every time that happens, I feel like a horrible beast."

Was he still talking about Sammy, or was he referring to her reaction by the door? She must not ask.

"Sammy has had a lot of changes in his life over the past couple of days. He was too wound up today to take a nap, so he's overly tired, too."

"At least he's happy to spend time with Deborah."

"And she with him." She started to add more, but put her hand to the side of her belly when the *boppli* kicked. "Ouch!"

"A strong one?" he asked.

She smiled. "It kicks like a horse. Maybe it's warning me that I won't get much chance to sit once it's born. When I'm busy, it's quiet. As soon as I take a moment's rest, it begins its footrace."

"Do you have names chosen?"

She shook her head, not wanting to hear his next words. The ones everyone said. If it was a boy, surely she would name it for its late *daed*. How could she explain Lloyd was the last name she would select? Without being honest about the man he'd been, she would sound petty and coldhearted.

"Don't let the *kinder* know," he said, startling her with his smile. "You'll be bombarded with more name suggestions than you could use for a dozen litters of kittens. I doubt the names Mittens and Spot would be of much use to you."

She laughed honestly and freely. The sound burst out of a place within her she'd kept silent for so long she'd almost forgotten it existed. Tears teased the corners of her eyes. Not tears of pain or fear but tears of joy.

"That's a nice sound," he said, his smile growing wider. "It gives me hope that we're going to make this marriage work better than either of us can guess right now."

"I hope so."

"And to that end..." He moved to the other rocking chair. When he began to ask about her daily schedule and if she wanted him to pick up the few groceries they'd need from his brother's store or if she preferred to do the shopping herself, his questions showed he had many of the same anxieties she did, along with the determination to overcome them.

She answered each question the best she could. She had some of her own, which he replied to with a smile. More than once he mentioned he was glad she had thought of some matter he hadn't. His words made her feel part of the family, not an outsider who'd come to cook and clean and watch over the youngsters.

By the time they rose to go inside and spend time with the *kinder*, her shoulders felt lighter. She brought Sammy to sit beside her on a bench not far from the stove that would warm the room next winter. With her arm around him, she watched Joshua don a pair of dark-rimmed glasses. She'd had no idea he needed glasses.

Joshua read from Psalm 146, and she was comforted by the words of praise. "Happy is he that hath the God of Jacob for his help, whose hope is in the Lord his God... The Lord preserveth the strangers, He relieveth the fatherless and widow..."

She stroked her son's hair while he fell asleep. Holding him, she listened as Joshua continued. His warm voice rose and fell with the joyous words, and she found her own eyes growing heavy as she let the sound soothe her.

This was the future she'd imagined when she had accepted Lloyd's proposal. Evenings with the family gathered together, savoring the words inspired by God's love. The perfect end to the day as the gas lamp hissed and the last light of the day faded into night. An affirmation of faith and love with the people who were in her heart.

It wasn't perfect. Her marriage to Joshua wasn't a true one. However, there was no reason they couldn't work together to make a *gut* and happy home. He had treated her with kindness, and she prayed she'd seen the real man and that he had no secret life as Lloyd had.

After Joshua finished reading and the family prayed together, Rebekah took Sammy into the downstairs bedroom while Joshua and his *kinder* went upstairs. Their footfalls sounded along with the occasional creaking board while she settled her son into bed. He roused enough to ask for Spot, the stuffed dog he slept with each night. Telling him to stay where he was, she went into the dark kitchen. She used the flashlight she'd found in a drawer earlier, but had no luck finding Spot.

Sammy had had the stuffed toy with him when they'd gone upstairs that afternoon. Maybe he'd left it up there somewhere. If she hurried she could retrieve it before the other *kinder* were asleep.

After pausing to tell Sammy she would bring Spot to him in a few minutes, she went up the stairs far more slowly than Deborah and Levi had a few minutes ago. Gas lamps were on in the two bedrooms on the right side of the hallway. From beyond the first door to the left, she heard water splashing and guessed someone was brushing his or her teeth.

She glanced into Deborah's room. It was empty, and a quick scan told her Sammy's precious toy wasn't there. Maybe in the room the boys shared...

As she went to look there, a voice came from the half open door on the other side of the hall. Low, deep and fraught with pain. She froze when she realized it belonged to Joshua.

She should back away, but she couldn't move. She

saw Joshua sitting on the bed with his back to her. His head was bowed, and, at first, she thought he was praying. Then she realized he held something in his hands.

A rag rug that was frayed with wear around the edges.

He held it as if the worn fabric was a treasured lifeline. His gaze was so focused on the rug he was oblivious to everything else, even the fact his door had come ajar.

Go! she told herself, but her legs refused to work.

"Tildie, I hope you understand why I've done what I have," Joshua said. "I know you'd want our *kinder* to have the best care, and Rebekah is already giving them that. You told Lloyd often that he was blessed to have her as his wife. He was, and I am blessed to have her help and to be able to help her. But I miss having you here, Tildie. Nobody will ever take your place. Even if I can't show it any longer in public now that I'm married again, I'll never stop loving you."

The pain in his words matched what twisted through her heart. Her hope Joshua would be open and honest with her was dashed. So easily he spoke of keeping his love for his late wife a secret.

Secrets! They had dominated her first marriage. Now they dashed her hopes for her second one.

She edged away and pressed back against the wall so not even her shadow would betray her presence. Eavesdropping was wrong, especially during such a private conversation.

She walked away as quietly as she had come up the stairs. She knew it would be silly to run away as she longed to. She could fall and hurt herself on the stairs.

When she looked in the bedroom to check on Sammy,

she saw him curled up in bed, his toy in his arms. He must have remembered where he'd left it and gotten it on his own. She blinked back abrupt tears. The way Sammy cuddled with his precious Spot reminded her of how Joshua had held the torn rag rug with such love and sadness. A peculiar sensation surged through her.

Envy.

Envy that Joshua's love for his wife had survived even after her death, while Lloyd's had vanished as soon as he had had that first drink after their wedding. She wondered what it would be like to be loved like Joshua loved his Tildie and if she'd ever find out for herself.

Chapter Six

"Gute mariye!"

Joshua's *mamm* called out the greeting. Deborah rushed to hug her *grossmammi*. Wiping her hand on a towel, Rebekah smiled at Wanda Stoltzfus. The older woman's casted arm was wrapped in a black sling, but her eyes twinkled as she handed a basket topped with a blue cloth to her granddaughter.

During the two weeks since the wedding, the *kinder* had often visited the house down the road where Wanda lived with her six unmarried sons and younger daughter. Rebekah and Joshua and Sammy had been invited along with the rest of the family to dinner one night last week, but a bad storm had kept them at home. At church services on Sunday, Rebekah had appreciated her mother-in-law introducing her again to people she'd met at the wedding. She hoped she'd match names and faces better when the next church Sunday came around.

The past fourteen days had been a whirlwind. The lives of Joshua's family and her own had fallen into a pattern with meals and work and family time in the evening, but Rebekah avoided spending time on the porch—or anywhere else—alone with her husband. If he'd noticed, he hadn't said anything. Perhaps he was relieved she expected no more from him.

"Wanda, why are you waiting for an invitation?" Rebekah asked, glad a visitor gave her the excuse to think of something other than her peculiar marriage. "Come in, come in."

Putting her arm around her granddaughter, Wanda walked in. Her expression softened when her gaze alighted on Sammy.

"How is our big boy?" she asked.

Sammy clutched Rebekah's skirt. She scooped him up and settled him on her hip. He pressed his face against her shoulder.

Wanda winked at Rebekah before she said, "I hope you don't hide too long, my boy. Chocolate chip cookies are best when they're warm."

He didn't look up, but shifted so he could watch what the others did. The cookies smelled *wunderbaar*, and she guessed he was wavering between his shyness and his yearning for a treat.

"Deborah, will you unpack the basket?" Rebekah asked, earning a wide grin from the little girl. "Wanda, would you like to sit down?"

"*Ja*. This cast feels like it weighs more every day." She sat at the table and grimaced as she readjusted her arm. "I thank God I broke my left arm, though I had no idea how much I did with that hand until I couldn't use it."

"I discovered that when I broke my finger." She fought to keep her smile from wavering as the brutality of her past poked out to darken the day. "I appreciate you coming for a visit."

"I wanted to give you time to become accustomed to your new home." She looked around. "I'd say you are settling in well and making this a home again."

Deborah piped up, "She's teaching me to make lots of yummy things, *Grossmammi*."

"So I hear from your brothers." She winked at Rebckah. "Maybe I'll even share the recipe for my chocolate chip cookies with her."

"And me?" asked the little girl.

"Of course." She wagged a finger at the *kind*. "As long as you listen to me and don't try to make up your own recipes as you used to."

"*Daed* always did that."

"And how did it turn out?"

When Deborah burst into giggles, Rebekah laughed, too. "Let me heat some water, and we'll have tea. Deborah, would you mind getting the tea down?"

The little girl pulled a chair beside the cupboard and climbed up to take out a box of teabags.

As she turned to put on the kettle, Rebekah almost stumbled. She tightened her hold on Sammy.

"Give him to me," Wanda urged.

She doubted he would go to Wanda. "I don't want him to bump your injured arm."

"He won't."

"He's shy."

"So I see, but, Sammy, I know you want one of my chocolate chip cookies."

Her son astonished her when, after a quick glance at Wanda, he stretched out his arms to her. Hoping her face didn't reveal her surprise, Rebekah placed him on the older woman's lap. Wanda pointed to the plate on the table beside her.

"I've never met a boy who didn't like chocolate chip cookies." Wanda smiled when Sammy reached past her to take a cookie. "What a *gut* boy you are! Only taking one."

"More?" he asked.

"Why don't you try this one?" the older woman asked. "Tell me if you like *Grossmammi* Wanda's cookies."

"*Grossmammi* Wanda," he repeated as he stared at the cast. "Boo-boo?"

"*Ja*, but it is getting better."

"Give kiss to make better?"

"Aren't you a sweet little boy?" She nodded and tapped her cheek. "Why don't you kiss me right here?"

Rebekah was surprised when Sammy did. After serving tea to her mother-in-law, Rebekah gave the *kinder* glasses of milk. She sat and joined the easy conversation about the end of the school year, two new babies in the district and Deborah's friend Mandy, who seemed to be a favorite of Wanda's, too, because the little girl was often at the house. Nothing strayed too close to the unusual circumstances of Rebekah's marriage. Like her son, Rebekah grew comfortable with the kind older woman.

As soon as he'd finished his first cookie, Sammy had another and downed his milk with a gulp. He nodded when Rebekah asked him if he wanted more, then he looked across the table.

"Debbie!" He pointed with his cookie. "Milk, too?"

"*Ja*." Deborah grinned. "*Danki*, Sammy."

Rebekah refilled both glasses. "It sounds as if you've got a new name."

"He has trouble saying my whole name. So now we're Sammy and Debbie."

Wanda nodded. "That sounds perfect for a sister and brother."

"I have lots of brothers now." The little girl leaned on the table. "Rebekah, please have a girl."

Though she secretly harbored the same hope, Rebekah replied, "We shall be blessed with the *boppli* God has chosen for us." Even at her darkest times while she had been pregnant with Sammy, she hadn't doubted God was sending her a *boppli* to help ease her heart.

Before anyone could reply, the back door opened, and Joshua walked in. He smiled as he hung his straw hat on the peg by the door.

Her heart quivered, missing a beat when his gaze met hers. A warmth she'd never felt before swirled within her like a welcome breeze on a hot day. His light blue shirt bore the stains from his work at the buggy shop, and more grease was ingrained across his hands, emphasizing his roughened skin. She had always considered him a *gut*-looking man, but as his eyes crinkled with his broadening smile, she could not keep from thinking that he was now her *gut*-looking husband.

But he wasn't. Theirs wasn't a true marriage. It was an arrangement to ensure Sammy and his *kinder* were taken care of. Her head knew that, but not her heart that continued to pound against her breastbone.

"I didn't realize you were here, *Mamm*," Joshua said after greeting them.

"Your sister is cleaning the house, and she made it clear I was in the way." She smiled to take any sting from her words. "She's so worried I'll slip and break something else."

"Because you try to do everything as you did before you broke your arm." He reached across the table and snagged a pair of cookies.

"One," Sammy scolded. "Only one."

Rebekah's heart faltered again, but for a very different reason. Lloyd never tolerated his son telling him what to do. How would Joshua react to being scolded by a toddler? She clenched her hands. If he raised his hand to strike Sammy, she would protect her son.

But Joshua chuckled. "You're right, Sammy. One cookie at a time. But *Grossmammi*'s cookies are *gut*, aren't they?"

Sammy smiled and nodded. When he picked up his glass that was coated with crumbs, he offered it to Joshua.

After taking it, Joshua pretended to drink before saying, "*Danki*, Sammy. Just what I needed."

Her son's smile glowed. Rebekah looked from him to her husband. Was Sammy sensing, as he had with Wanda, that he had nothing to fear from Joshua?

"What are you doing home in the middle of the day?" Wanda asked. "Come to see your pretty new wife?"

"*Ja*, and my pretty daughter." He winked at Deborah, who giggled. "I told Levi I'd stop by on my way back from dropping off a repaired buggy. He's riding in with me so he can help Daniel at his shop."

"How is Daniel doing with him?" his *mamm* asked.

"Well. Having someone to teach has given my little brother a purpose."

"He is a *gut*, hardworking boy, but he's avoiding decisions he should make about joining the church and finding a wife." Wanda sighed. "I shouldn't feel *hoch-*

mut that four of my *kinder* so far have made the decision to be Amish."

"It isn't pride, *Mamm*." Joshua patted her right shoulder carefully. "You want what is best for each of us."

"True." Wanda smiled again. "And it sounds as if Daniel teaching Levi is *gut* for both of them."

"Levi is eager to learn. I wish I could say the same about his brother." He glanced at the two *kinder*. "Deborah, will you take Sammy outside and wash the cookie crumbs off his hands and face?"

"Ja," she replied, though her expression said she'd prefer to stay.

As soon as the *kinder* had closed the door after them, Joshua sighed. "I could use some advice, *Mamm*. Timothy is growing less and less interested in learning about buggies."

Rebekah went to get a dishrag to scrub off the cookie crumbles that would grow as hard as concrete if left on the table. She listened as Joshua and Wanda discussed Timothy's reluctance to do anything at the shop. Not even building wheels, a task he used to look forward to, engaged his attention now.

She should say nothing. Timothy wasn't her son, and, other than being enthusiastic about the food she put on the table, he hadn't said much to her. She seldom saw him other than at breakfast and dinner. He was with Joshua during the day, and he always seemed to be somewhere else once the evening meal was over. He came in for Joshua's nightly reading from the Bible or *Martyrs Mirror*, but vanished again after their prayers.

"I don't know what else I can tell you," Wanda said with a sigh. "You've tried everything I would have."

"Having every day be one long debate about what I

need him to do is getting old very fast." Joshua ran his fingers through his beard and looked at Rebekah. "Do you have any ideas?"

"Timothy does his share of chores here, doesn't he?" she asked, choosing her words carefully. Joshua might not like what she was about to say, but he'd asked her opinion.

"*Ja.*"

"Without complaint?"

"Usually." His brows lowered with bafflement. "What does that have to do with his attitude at the buggy shop?"

"Maybe Timothy doesn't show any interest in your work because it isn't the work he wants to do."

Joshua stared as if she'd suggested he flap his arms and fly around the yard. "I plan to hand the business over to him when I am ready to retire."

"It's *your* plan. Not his." She met his gaze steadily.

Wanda stood and patted Rebekah's arm. "Now I'm even more glad you're a part of our family. You have put your finger on the crux of the problem." She looked at her son. "Have you asked Timothy if he wants to take over the shop?"

"No." He drew in a deep breath and let it out slowly. "I assumed because he used to be curious about what I was doing that he wanted to learn the work himself."

"He was a *kind*," his *mamm* said with a gentle smile. "As his *daed*, you were what he wanted to be when he grew up. Now he is nearly a man, and he sees the world and himself differently." She made a shooing motion with her fingers. "You need to talk with your son, and it's not going to get easier by putting it off."

"True." Joshua's tone was so dreary his *mamm*

laughed. When he began to chuckle along with her, Rebekah joined in.

She'd forgotten how *wunderbaar* shared laughter could be. She hoped she wouldn't have to forget again.

The rumble of a powerful engine surprised Rebekah. Turning from where she was folding the quilts she had aired, she stared at the bright red car slowing to a stop not far from the house. She grabbed Sammy's hand when he took a step toward it.

"Go! See!" he shouted.

She was about to reply when Timothy ran around the house and toward the car. She hadn't realized he was home yet.

The driver's window rolled down, and Timothy leaned forward to fold his arms on the open sill. She heard him laugh and wondered if it was the first time she'd ever heard him do so.

After dropping the quilt in the laundry basket, she began to cross the yard to where the teen was now squatting so his face was even with whoever was inside the car. She absently pushed loose wisps back under her *kapp*, because she wasn't sure who was behind the wheel.

Deborah skipped down the front porch steps. She'd been beating dust out of rag rugs. She waited for Rebekah and walked with her toward the vehicle.

Rebekah's eyes widened when she realized the driver was an *Englisch* girl, one close to Timothy's age. The girl's black hair was pulled back in a ponytail. Unlike many *Englisch* teenagers, she wasn't wearing layers of makeup. She didn't need any because her lightly tanned cheeks were a healthy pink. She wore a simple and modest black blouse.

"I'm Alexis Granger," said the girl. "Hey, Tim, move back so I can see your new mom." She laughed, and Timothy did, too. Leaning her elbow on the car's open window, she said, "You must be Joshua's new wife."

Startled by the *Englisch* girl's effusiveness, Rebekah smiled. "*Ja*, I am Rebekah." She looked at Sammy who was eyeing the girl and the car with the same interest Timothy was. "And this is my son Samuel."

"A big name for a cute, little boy."

"We call him Sammy."

The pretty brunette chuckled. "Much better. Hi, Sammy."

He gave her a shy grin but didn't say anything.

"He's a real cutie," Alexis said before holding out a stack of envelopes. "These were delivered to our mailbox by mistake, and Mom asked me to drop them off over here on my way to work."

"Where do you work?" Rebekah asked to be polite.

"At one of the diners in Bird-in-Hand where the tourists come to try Amish-style food." She hooked a thumb in Timothy's direction. "*He* thinks I got the job because my boss was impressed my neighbors are plain, but it was because I was willing to work on weekends." She rolled her eyes. "Saving for college, y'know. Anything I can pick up for you while I'm in town?"

"*Danki*, but we're fine."

"Okay. See ya, Tim!" She backed the car out onto the road. Small stones spurted from under the back tires.

Rebekah half turned to protect Sammy. Even though the tiny stones didn't come near them, a dust cloud billowed over them.

The glow that had brightened Timothy's face while Alexis was there faded. Without a word, he walked back to the house. As he did, he tucked his fingers into one side of his suspenders and tugged at them on each step, clearly deep in thought.

"Don't mind him," Deborah said, warning Rebekah she'd stared too long. "He's like that when Alexis stops by."

"She comes often?"

"*Ja*, but not as much as she used to. She's always got something going on at school or at work. Timothy misses having her around. He thinks she's hot."

Shocked, Rebekah began, "Deborah—"

"Will you call me Debbie as Sammy does?" the little girl asked with a grin.

"We'll talk about your name in a minute. You shouldn't make such comments about Alexis. It isn't nice."

The girl frowned. "Timothy said it was a compliment."

"I'm sure he did, but your brother hasn't learned yet that what's inside a person is more important than the outside."

"But *Daedi* said *you're* pretty when he told us he was going to marry you."

Rebekah ignored the delight that sprang through her, but it wasn't easy. "He and I have known each other for years. He didn't marry me for what I look like." She put her hands on her distended belly. "Certainly not now!"

That brought a laugh from the little girl, and Rebekah changed the subject to the chores they had left to do before Joshua and Levi got home.

As Deborah turned to head back to the front porch, she asked, "Will you call me Debbie?"

"As long as your *daed* agrees. He'll want you to have a *gut* reason."

The little girl considered her words for a long minute, then said, "I want to be called Debbie so Sammy feels part of our family."

Unbidden tears filled Rebekah's eyes. What a *wunderbaar* heart Debbie had been blessed with! As she assured Debbie she would speak with Joshua about the nickname after dinner, she had to keep blinking to keep those tears from falling. She hugged the *kind*.

Dearest God, danki *for bringing this little girl into my life.* Sweet Debbie was making Sammy a part of her family, and Rebekah, too. For the first time in longer than she could remember, Rebekah felt the burden she carried on her shoulders every day lift. It was an amazing feeling she wanted to experience again and again. Was it finally possible?

Joshua heard the screen door open after supper, but he kept reading the newspaper's sports section. The last light of the day was beginning to fade, and he wanted to finish the article on the new pitcher who had signed with the Phillies. He'd been following the Philadelphia baseball team since he wasn't much older than Sammy. His sons were baseball fans, too, and he'd expected Timothy or Levi to come out and ask for an update before now.

When a question wasn't fired in his direction, he looked up. His eyes widened when he saw Rebekah standing there.

Alone.

The last time she'd spent any time with him without one of the *kinder* nearby was the first evening when they'd tried to work out aspects of their marriage. How guilty he'd felt afterward! Though he knew his life was now entwined with Rebekah's, his heart belonged to Tildie. He wanted to be a *gut* husband, but how could he when he needed to hold on to his love for the first woman he had exchanged vows with?

My brother, do you take our sister to be your wife until such hour as when death parts you? Do you believe this is the Lord's will, and your prayers and faith have brought you to each other?

The words Reuben had asked him at the wedding ceremony rang through his head. They were identical to the vows he had taken with Tildie. Why hadn't anyone told him how he was supposed to act once death parted him from Tildie? The *Ordnung* outlined many other parts of their lives. Why not that?

Renewed guilt rushed through him when he saw Rebekah regarding him with uncertainty. She must be enduring the same feeling of being lost without Lloyd, though she never gave any sign. Perhaps she was trying to spare him.

"I'm sorry if I've disturbed your reading," she said. "The *kinder* are practicing their parts for the end-of-the-school-year program next week. Sammy is their rapt audience."

He chuckled. "The end-of-the-school-year program is important to them. It's hard to think how few more Levi will be in. At least there will be others with Deborah and Sammy."

"I thought you should know Deborah wants to be called Debbie now."

"Why?"

Her soft blue eyes glistened as she told him how his daughter longed to help Sammy feel more at home with his new family. Were those tears, or was it a trick of the light?

His own voice was a bit rough when he said, "Debor—Debbie has always been thoughtful. I wish I could say the same for her older brother."

"May I talk to you about Timothy?"

He lowered the newspaper to his lap and lifted off his reading glasses. "Has he been giving you trouble?"

"No," she said as she sat in the rocker. "He treats me politely."

"I'm glad to hear that." He didn't add he'd worried his older son would take out his frustrations with his *daed* on Rebekah. He was jolted when he realized that unlike his younger siblings, Timothy had perceived the distance between the newlyweds.

Was it obvious to everyone?

He didn't have a chance to answer the unanswerable because Rebekah said, "But I have noticed something about Timothy that concerns me."

"What?" He silenced his sigh. After trying to motivate his son to do something other than mope around the buggy shop, he didn't want to deal with Timothy again tonight.

Instantly he chided himself. A parent's job didn't end when the workday did. Because he was worried about his failure to reconnect with the boy who once dogged his footsteps was no reason to give up. His son was trying to find his place in the world, as every teenager did.

"Have you noticed," Rebekah asked, drawing his attention back to her, "how Timothy stops whatever he's doing whenever Alexis Granger and her snazzy car goes by?"

"Snazzy?"

"It's a word, right?"

He smiled. "It is, and it's the perfect description for the car. I know Brad wishes he'd gotten a less powerful one. Letting a new driver like Alexis get behind the wheel is like giving Sammy the reins to our family buggy."

"I'm not as worried about the car as I am about Timothy's interest in it…and the girl who drives it."

"They've been friends since they were little more than babies."

"But they aren't babies any longer." She sighed. "I don't want to cause trouble, Joshua, but Timothy lit up like a falling star when she was here, and I noticed him watching her go the whole way up the Grangers' driveway tonight. As soon as supper was over, he was gone."

"Saturday nights are for him to be with his friends."

"I realize that, but Alexis fascinates him. If you want my opinion…"

"I do."

She met his eyes evenly. "He'd like more than a friendship with her."

Joshua folded his glasses and put them on the windowsill by his chair. He did the same with the newspaper as he considered her words. Maybe he had been turning too blind an eye toward his oldest's friendship with the neighbor girl. He didn't want to do anything to cause his son to retreat further from the family. To confront Timothy about the matter could create more problems.

When Rebekah didn't say more, he was grateful. She

wasn't going to nag him about his son as his older sister Ruth did. Ruth's *kinder* didn't seem to have a rebellious bone in their bodies, so she couldn't understand what it was like to have a son like Timothy. But he'd think about what Rebekah had said.

"*Danki* for caring enough for my son to be worried about him," he said, reaching out to put his hand on hers.

She moved her fingers so smoothly he wouldn't have noticed if he hadn't seen her flinch away too many times. As she came to her feet, unable to hide that she wanted to put more space between them, she said, "I'm not Timothy's *mamm*, but I care about him."

Do you care about me, too? The question went unasked, and it would remain unasked, because he realized how much he wanted the answer to be *ja* and how much he feared it would be no.

Chapter Seven

The yard of the simple, white schoolhouse at the intersection of two country roads was filled with buggies, and more were pulling in as Rebekah climbed the steps after Joshua. She was glad Sammy could manage the steps on his own, because it was more difficult each day to pick him up and carry him. Inside, the schoolroom looked almost identical to the one she had attended. The same textbooks were on the shelves at the back of the room, and the scholars' desks were set in neat rows with the teacher's desk at the front of the blackboard.

An air of anticipation buzzed through the room. The scholars were eager to begin their program as well as their summer break. Younger *kinder* looked around, excited to get a glimpse of where they would be attending school. Parents used the gathering as a chance to catch up on news.

Most of the *mamms* sat at the scholars' desks, but Rebekah decided to remain at the back with the *daeds* and grandparents and other relatives. She was unsure if her ever-widening belly would fit behind one of the small desks.

The room was filled with sunshine, but its glow wasn't as bright as the smiles on the scholars' faces while they stood near their teacher's desk. On the blackboard behind them, someone—probably Esther Stoltzfus, their teacher—had written in big block letters: HAVE A FUN AND SAFE SUMMER!

Joshua's younger sister looked happy and harried at the same time. Levi and Debbie talked with fondness and respect for their teacher who was also their *aenti*. Now Esther was trying to get each of the scholars in the proper place for the beginning of the program. The youngest ones complied quickly, but the oldest ones, knowing this was their final day of school, seemed unable to stand still or stop talking and giggling.

But Esther treated each *kind* with patience and a smile. When two of the younger scholars went to her and whispered below the buzz of conversation in the room, she nodded. They ran out the side door and toward the outhouses at the back corner of the schoolyard.

After she turned to scan the room, Esther smiled warmly when her eyes met Rebekah's. She went to her desk and pulled out her chair. She rolled it to the back of the room and stopped by Rebekah.

Esther motioned at the chair. "Would you like to sit down?"

"I don't want to take your chair."

"I won't have a chance to sit." Her dimples rearranged the freckles scattered across her cheeks and nose. "Please use it."

"Danki." She wasn't going to turn down the *gut*-hearted offer a second time.

Joshua took the back of the chair from his sister and

shifted it closer to the last row of desks. "You should be able to see better from here, Rebekah."

"Danki," she repeated as she sat with a relieved sigh. She settled Sammy on her knees. While the men talked about farming and the weather and the latest news on their favorite baseball teams, she pointed out the posters and hand-drawn pictures tacked on cork strips that hung about a foot below the ceiling. He was delighted with each one and asked when he could come to school with the older *kinder.* With a smile, she assured him it would be soon.

When the two young scholars returned, they took their places. Rebekah smiled when she saw Debbie at the far right in the front row of girls while Levi peered over the head of the scholar in front of him from the other end of the back row.

"Debbie! Levi!" called Sammy as the room became silent.

Everyone laughed, and Rebekah whispered to him that he needed to be quiet so he could hear the songs.

Sammy bounced on Rebekah's knees as the *kinder* began to sing. He clapped along with the adults at the end of each song. The recitations made him squirm with impatience, but each time another song began, he tried to join in with a tuneless, "La, la, la."

Rebekah enjoyed the program and was pleased when Debbie and Levi performed their poems without a single hesitation or mistake. She glanced up to see Joshua smiling. Though pride wasn't considered a *gut* thing among the Amish, she could tell he enjoyed seeing his *kinder* do well after their hard work to memorize each word.

Sammy grew bored during a short play performed

by the oldest scholars. Other toddlers were wiggling and looking around, as well. Even a cookie couldn't convince him to sit still.

"Down," he said. When she didn't react, he repeated it more loudly.

Not wanting him to disrupt the program, she let him slide off her knees. She whispered for him to stay by her side.

"Hold hand?" he asked.

She nodded and held out her hand. She was astonished when he took Joshua's fingers. Leaning his head against Joshua's leg, he smiled when her husband tousled his hair without taking his eyes off the program.

Sammy obviously had changed his mind about Joshua. A warm glow filled her. She'd seen signs of the change in recent days, but her son had remained tentative around Joshua in public. For the first time, he wasn't clinging to her.

Her joy disappeared when Sammy suddenly darted past her as the *kinder* began to sing again. She jumped to her feet, but he grasped Debbie's hand and announced, "Sammy sing, too."

Rebekah's face burned as she started toward the *kinder* who were giggling at her son's antics. Her sneaker caught, and a broad hand grasped her shoulder, halting her. Time telescoped into the past to the night Lloyd had kept her from leaving the house by seizing her from behind and shoving her against a wall. Her reaction was instinctive.

Her arm came up to knock her captor's hand away. "No! Don't!" she gasped and whirled away so fast she bumped into a desk and almost tumbled off her feet.

Hands from the people around her steadied her. She

was grateful, but as panic drained away, she saw startled and alarmed expressions on all the faces around her.

No, not *all* the faces. Joshua's was as blank as the wall behind him. He stood with his arm still outstretched. To keep her from falling, she realized. His eyes contained a myriad of emotions. Mixed in with confusion and annoyance was…hurt. A new wife shouldn't shy away from her husband's touch. She had embarrassed him in front of his family and neighbors. If she could explain without risking Sammy's future…

Esther's cheerful voice sounded forced. "Let's start over with our final song of this year's program. Sammy and any of the other younger *kinder* are welcome to join us."

While more little brothers and sisters rushed up to stand beside their siblings, Rebekah groped for her chair. Joshua steadied it as she sat, but she couldn't speak, not even to thank him. She lowered herself to sit and stared straight ahead.

Sammy now stood beside Levi in the back row with the other boys. As the *kinder* enthusiastically sang their friendship song, he looked up at Levi with admiration and tried to sing along, though he didn't know the words.

It was endearing, but she couldn't enjoy it. Adrenaline rushed through her, making her gasp as if she had run a marathon. Her pulse thudded in her ears so loudly she had to strain to hear the *kinder*'s voices. She clapped along with everyone else when the song came to an end.

The *kinder* scattered, seeking their parents. Hugs and excited voices filled the schoolroom.

Rebekah pushed herself to her feet again when Levi, Debbie and Sammy eased along an aisle to where she and Joshua waited. She hoped her smile didn't look hideous while she thanked the *kinder* for a *wunderbaar* program. If her voice was strained, the youngsters didn't seem to notice.

However, the adults around her must have. More than one gave her a smile. Not pitying, but sympathetic, especially the women who carried small babies. Their kindness and concern was almost too great a gift to accept.

And, she realized, nobody looked toward Joshua with censure. None of them could imagine him hurting her on purpose. That thought should have been comforting, but who would have guessed Lloyd could be a beast when he drank? She certainly hadn't.

She'd made one mistake. Now she wanted to avert another, but would the mistake be trusting Joshua or not trusting him?

The schoolyard was filled with happy shouts and lighthearted conversation. Everywhere, including where Joshua stood with his family. The noise came from the *kinder*, who were as agitated as if they'd eaten a whole batch of their *grossmammi's* cookies. But he was glad no one paid attention to the fact neither he nor Rebekah said anything as they walked with their *kinder* to the buggy. Everyone was too wound up in happiness to notice his misery.

And Rebekah's?

He wasn't sure what she was thinking or feeling. She hid it behind a strained smile.

What happened? he wanted to shout, though he seldom raised his voice. Nothing could be gained by yelling and things could be lost, but his frustration was reaching the boiling point.

He hesitated as he was about to assist Rebekah into the buggy. Would she pull away as she had in the schoolhouse? Humiliation burned in his gut as he recalled the curious glances aimed in his direction, glances quickly averted.

But stronger than his chagrin was his need to know why she'd acted as she had. Until she'd pulled away from him, he'd thought they were becoming accustomed to each other and had found a compromise that allowed them to make a *gut* and comfortable home for the *kinder*. He had dared to believe, even though theirs was far from a perfect marriage, it had the potential to become a comfortable one.

Now he wasn't sure about anything.

God, help me. Help us! Something is wrong, and I don't know what it is.

Wondering if he really had anything to lose, Joshua offered his hand to Rebekah, and she accepted it as if nothing unusual had happened. As the *kinder*, including Sammy, scrambled into the back, he stepped in, as well. He picked up the reins and slapped them against the horse.

Rebekah remained silent, but he doubted she would have had a chance to speak when the *kinder* chattered like a flock of jays rising from a field. Sammy was eager to learn the words to the final song they had sung, and Debbie was trying to teach him while Levi described every bit of the program as if none of them had been there. They kept interrupting each other to ask him and Rebekah if they'd liked one part of it or another.

He answered automatically. Every inch of him was focused on the woman sitting beside him. Her fingers quivered, and he was tempted to put his own hand over them to remind her, whatever was distressing her, she wasn't alone in facing it. He resisted.

The *kinder* rushed out of the buggy as soon as it stopped beside the house. When Rebekah slid away and got out on her side, he jumped out and called her name. She turned as he unhooked the horse from the buggy.

"Come with me and Benny," Joshua said simply.

"I should…" She met his gaze and then nodded. "All right."

She walked on the other side of the horse as they went to the barn. She waited while he put Benny in a stall and gave him some oats.

He stepped out of the stall. "Rebekah—"

"Joshua—" she said at the same time.

"Go ahead," he urged.

"Danki." She paused so long he wondered if she'd changed her mind about speaking. He realized she'd been composing her thoughts when she said, "I don't know any other way to say this but I'm sorry I embarrassed you at school. I will apologize to Esther the next time I see her."

"Rebekah, if I was embarrassed or not isn't important. What's important is why you said what you did. Tell me the truth. Why did you pull away like you did?"

"Haven't you heard pregnant women often act strangely?" Her smile wobbled, and he guessed she was exerting her flagging strength to keep it in place.

"Ja, but…" He didn't want to accuse her of lying. Not that she was, but she was avoiding the truth. Why? "I was trying to prevent you from falling."

"I know." Her voice had a soft breathlessness that urged him closer, but her face was stiff with the fear he'd seen at school. "I need to be careful I avoid doing anything that might injure my *boppli*."

Maybe he'd misread her reaction, and her anxiety about the *boppli* had made her words sound wrong. He hadn't always been correct in his assumptions about Tildie's reactions, either.

The thought startled him. Since Tildie's death he hadn't let such memories into his mind. At first he'd felt ungrateful if he recalled anything but the *gut* times they'd shared. Even a jest from his brothers about married life had fallen flat for him. He didn't want to admit, even to himself, his marriage to Tildie had been anything less than perfect.

But that was the past. He had to focus on keeping his current marriage from falling apart before it even had a chance to thrive. He refused to believe it was already too late.

"One of the reasons I asked you to be my wife is to make sure you and your *kinder* are taken care of," he said as he walked with her out of the barn. "I told you that right from the beginning."

"I know you did."

"Do you believe I was being honest?"

When she paused and faced him, he was surprised. He'd expected her to try to keep distance between them. Now they stood a hand's breadth from each other. She tilted her head enough so he could see her face beneath her bonnet's brim. Even as she drew in a breath to speak, he wondered if he could remember how to breathe as he gazed into her beautiful blue eyes.

"I believe you aspire to being as honest as any man can be, Joshua Stoltzfus," she whispered.

"Then believe I don't want you to worry about you

and your *kinder*. I take my vows seriously to face every challenge with you, Rebekah. God has brought us together, and I believe His plans are always for *gut*."

"I do, too."

"It pleases me to hear you say that." He admired the scattering of freckles that drew his gaze to the curve of her cheekbones and then to her full lips. His imagination sped faster than a runaway horse as he speculated how her red hair would brush her face and his fingertips if it fell, loose and untamed, down her back. She was his wife, and he'd thought often during the long nights since their wedding of her sitting in their bedroom and brushing out those long strands.

She was his wife, and he was her husband.

He framed her face with his hands before another thought could form. Her skin was soft and warm… and alive. How many times had he reached out in the past few years and found nothing but the chill of an old memory?

Her blue eyes beckoned but he hesitated. A man could lose himself within their depths. Was he ready to take the step from which there would be no turning back? The memory of Tildie and their love remained strong, and Rebekah's loss was still fresh and painful.

But didn't God want them to put others aside and cleave to one another, heart to heart, now that they were wed? The thought shook him. He wanted to live the life God had set out for him, but he hadn't been when he let the past overwhelm the present.

He saw her lips forming his name, but the sound never reached his ears as he bent toward her…toward his wife…his lovely Rebekah…

The squeal of tires on the road jerked him back to

reality, and he released her as Timothy strolled up the driveway whistling. His son grinned as he waved at Alexis who tooted the car's horn to him.

Joshua heard the kitchen door shut, and Rebekah was gone. He stood there with his hands empty. He had let his opportunity to hold her slip away. He prayed it wouldn't be his only chance.

Chapter Eight

A dozen contrasting emotions flooded Rebekah as the buggy entered the lane leading to the house where she used to live with Lloyd. It had been her home for more than five years, but the site of her greatest nightmare. Sammy had been born there and taken his first steps in the kitchen. It was also the place where Lloyd had first struck her in a drunken rage.

She hadn't expected Joshua to suggest a drive on the Saturday morning a week and a half after the school program. Previously on Saturdays he'd tended to chores in the barn or gone through catalogs to plan for what he needed to order for the buggy shop. Her heart had leaped with excitement because she'd hoped he was going to give her a tour of his shop. She wasn't sure why he hadn't asked her and Sammy to visit, but as each day passed, asking him seemed more difficult.

At first she'd needed to concentrate on getting the house back into acceptable shape. A stomach bug had made the three younger *kinder* sick and claimed her time and attention last week. As soon as they were well, Timothy had gotten sick. Yesterday was the first day he'd joined them for a meal, and he'd eaten no more than a few bites before he'd excused himself and returned to bed.

Keeping herself busy allowed her not to spend time alone with her husband. He hadn't said anything, but she knew he was curious why she continued to avoid him. If his son hadn't arrived when Joshua had clasped her face in his broad hands, he would have kissed her. What she didn't know was what would have happened if she'd kissed him back. The precarious balance of caring for the *kinder* at the same time she struggled not to care too much for her husband was a seesaw. A single step in the wrong direction could destroy that fragile equilibrium.

Now he had asked for her to go for a drive with him, and she'd accepted because she didn't have a *gut* excuse not to, especially because she liked spending time with him as long as they kept everything casual. She had been astonished when she learned their destination wasn't Joshua's buggy shop but Bird-in-Hand and Lloyd's farm. She'd agreed it was a *gut* idea to check on the house. When Joshua had told her that Timothy would bring the other *kinder* over in the open wagon after they finished their Saturday chores, she was grateful for her husband's thoughtfulness. She couldn't put any of the larger items she wanted to bring back to Paradise Springs in the family buggy, but they would fit easily in the wagon.

While they drove on Newport Road to bypass most of the busy tourist areas, she'd pointed out various landmarks. Joshua nodded as they passed the butcher's shop and suggested they stop on the way back to Paradise Springs, because his brother's store had a very small meat section with not a lot of items. She'd showed him the white schoolhouse Sammy would have attended and the medical clinic between a florist shop and a store selling quilts and Amish-built furniture.

"They've contacted my brother Jeremiah about selling some of his pieces there," he had said. "He's done well enough at our family's shops, but he's wavering. He likes the work, but not the paperwork that selling directly to customers requires." He looked at the medical clinic. "Shouldn't you be seeing a doctor for regular checkups?"

"I went before the wedding, and the midwife suggested I find another clinic in Paradise Springs. Is there one?"

"Ja," he had replied. "Do you want me to make an appointment for you?"

"That might be a *gut* idea."

He had changed the subject, but now neither she nor Joshua said anything as he brought the buggy to a stop near the kitchen door. He stepped out, and she did the same. She looked around.

Each inch of the house and the barns and the fields held a memory for her, *gut* and oh-so-bad. It was as if those memories were layered one atop another on the scene in front of her. The most recent ones of her and Sammy were the easiest, because they weren't laced with fright.

The farm had been her prison, but it had become a symbol for her freedom from fear since Lloyd's death. It still was, she realized in amazement. The farm was her sanctuary if she needed it. She didn't know if she would, but she wasn't going to be unprepared ever again.

Joshua crossed his arms over his light blue shirt. "What do you think?"

"About what?" She wasn't going to share the true course of her thoughts.

"The appearance of the farm. From what I can see, most of the buildings don't need much more than a coat or two of paint to make them look *gut*."

"I agree, except the roof on the field equipment barn is sagging. It should be shored up."

He gave her a warm smile. "True, and I know just the man for the job."

"Your brother Daniel?"

"*Ja*. He has repaired buildings in worse condition. I asked him to meet us here, so he can see what needs to be done. We want the buildings to look their best, so someone will offer a *gut* amount of money for the farm."

"Money for the farm?" she repeated, shocked at how easily he spoke of selling the farm. *Her farm!*

"*Ja*. Once it is fixed up, I thought we'd hold an auction for the land and buildings, as well as for anything else you want to sell—furniture, household goods and any farm equipment. Several neighbors have stopped by the buggy shop in the past couple of weeks to ask me when I plan to put it on the auction block, so the bidding should go well."

He was going to sell her farm. Just like that. Lloyd had insisted on making the big decisions, too, and she'd learned not to gainsay him. Why had she thought Joshua might be different?

Or maybe he wasn't the same as Lloyd. After all, Joshua had invited her to the farm to consider what needed to be done in order to sell it. He hadn't sold it without allowing her to see her home one more time.

The thought gave her the courage to say, "Joshua, I don't know if I'm ready to sell the farm yet."

"Why do you want to hold on to it?" He glanced from her to the weatherworn buildings. "If you're thinking you shouldn't sell it because it's Lloyd's legacy to Sammy, you need to consider how much upkeep it's going to need until he's old enough to farm. You could rent out the fields and the house, but buildings require regular upkeep, and it might cost as much or more than what you'd get from the rent. Selling the farm will provide money for Sammy when he's ready to decide what he wants to do as a man."

She knew he was right…about Sammy. But he had no idea about the true reason she couldn't bear to let the farm go. How she'd longed for a refuge when Lloyd had been looking for someone to blame for his ills! Nothing Joshua had done suggested he would be as abusive as her first husband, but she needed a place to go with Sammy if that changed.

Not just Sammy, but the other *kinder* if they needed shelter, too.

Rebekah hoped her shrug appeared nonchalant. "I hadn't thought about what would happen with the farm." That much was the truth. "I need time to think about selling it." Walking to where hostas were growing lush near the porch, she took the time to pray for the right words to persuade Joshua to listen.

From where he hadn't moved, he said, "It'll take time to repair the buildings, especially as Daniel will need to do the work around his other jobs. At this time of the summer we can't ask for others to help." He paused, then asked, "Rebekah?"

She faced him. *"Ja?"*

"You'll have plenty of time to make up your mind. You don't need to decide today." He gave her a cockeyed smile that made something uncurl delightfully in her center.

Something drew her toward him, something that urged her to think of his arms around her. She halted because she'd learned not to trust those feelings after they'd led her to Lloyd.

The rattle of the open wagon came from the end of the lane, and Rebekah saw Timothy driving the other *kinder* toward the house. As they neared, the older ones looked around, their eyes wide with astonishment. She guessed they were comparing their *onkel* Ezra's neat and well-maintained farm to this one.

But her gaze went to her son. She'd protected him from much of what had happened between her and his *daed*, and his young age would wash away other memories. Still, she didn't want this visit to upset him. She realized she didn't have anything to worry about when she heard his giggles as he played in the back of the wagon with Debbie.

Joshua lifted the younger *kinder* out while the boys jumped down. At the same time, he asked Rebekah where the lawnmower was. He sent Levi to get it from the shed. Timothy was given the task of collecting any canned food and other supplies from the kitchen and the cellar, while Debbie volunteered to look for any vegetables in the neglected garden.

"Sammy help?" her son asked.

"Help me," Timothy said, picking him up and hanging him upside down over his shoulder. While Sammy kicked his feet and chortled in delight, he added, "I'll keep a close eye on him in the kitchen, Rebekah. Before I go down to the cellar, I'll take him out to help Debbie."

"Danki." She didn't add how pleased she was Timo-

thy had volunteered to spend time with her son. It would be *gut* for both boys.

If Joshua was surprised by his oldest's actions, he didn't show it as he walked into the backyard. He went to the chicken coop, which she'd kept in excellent shape. It was the only building that had been painted in the past three years.

"Where are the chickens?" he asked as he looked over his shoulder.

"I gave the leftover chickens to my *mamm* so she can have fresh eggs." As she crossed the yard to where he stood, she rubbed her hands together, then stopped when she realized the motion showed her nervousness at being on the farm again. Maybe it wouldn't be the best haven.

But it was her only one.

She shivered and hastily added, "Most of the chickens were used for the wedding."

"I remember." He gave her a wry grin. "Though I don't remember much about what else we ate."

"I don't, either."

He paused and faced her. She took a half step back before she bumped into him. His mouth tightened. She'd given him every reason to believe a commonplace motion like trying not to run into someone had a great significance.

Before she could think of a way to explain, his expression eased again. He took her right hand between his and gazed into her eyes with a gentle honesty that threatened to demolish her resolve to keep her secrets to herself.

"What I do remember vividly," he said in little more than a whisper, "is how when you came down the stairs

I forgot everyone else in the room. I remember how you made sure my *kinder* didn't feel left out and how you welcomed them to participate in each tradition. Not many brides would have insisted on the *kinder* sharing our special corner during the wedding meal."

"Sammy was fussy, so I wanted to keep him nearby. How could I have had him there with us and not the others?"

"You don't need to explain, Rebekah. I'm simply saying I know our marriage isn't what either of us planned on, but —"

"It could be worse?"

When he laughed hard, she released a soft breath of relief. His words had become too serious, too sincere, too…everything. She couldn't let herself be swayed by pretty words as she had with Lloyd. Hadn't she learned her lesson? Even if Joshua wasn't like Lloyd, and she prayed every day he wasn't, she couldn't forget how he still loved his late wife.

"I don't want to farm this land or any other, Rebekah." He gave her a lopsided grin. "I know every Amish man is supposed to want to be a farmer, but I don't. God didn't give me the gifts he gave my brother. Ezra seems to know exactly when to plant and when to harvest. He can communicate with his herd of cows like he's one of them. That's why we agreed, rather than having the farm go to Daniel as the youngest son, Ezra should take over after *Daed* died. To be honest, Daniel was relieved, because he likes building things. It worked out well for each of us."

"It did."

He became serious again. "Rebekah, if you hoped

I'd farm here, I'm sorry. We probably should have discussed this before our wedding."

As well as so many other things, she wanted to say. But the most important truths must remain unspoken.

"*Danki* for being honest with me," she said. "No, I didn't expect you to take over the farm, especially when it's so far from your home and your shop." She didn't hesitate before she added, "I hope you'll invite me and Sammy to visit the shop one of these days."

His eyes grew wide. "You want to visit the buggy shop? I thought you weren't interested, because you haven't said anything about going there."

"Joshua, you love your work, and as your wife I want to understand what is important to you."

He smiled as broadly as Sammy did when offered a sweet. "Whenever you want to visit, drop in. I'll show you around so you can see how we make and repair buggies. Come as often as you wish."

When she saw how thrilled he was, happiness bubbled up within her from a hidden spring she thought had long ago gone dry. She felt closer to her husband than she ever had.

Had he sensed that, too? She couldn't think why else he would rapidly change the subject back to the condition of the farm buildings.

"Daniel should be here soon," he said. "The project he's been working on isn't far from here. If you see him, will you send him to the main barn? I'll start there."

"All right." She felt as if she'd been dismissed like a *kind* caught eavesdropping on her elders.

As she turned to go to the house, he added, "It's going to take time to get the buildings fixed up. Once everything is in decent shape, we'll talk about the future of the farm. Okay?"

"Ja," she said, though they were postponing the inevitable clash of wills. There must be some way to explain why she needed to keep the farm without revealing the truth about Lloyd.

But how?

Joshua watched as his youngest brother poked at a beam with a nail, and he tried not to sneeze as bits of hay and dust and spiderwebs drifted down onto his upturned face. Daniel was trying to determine if any insects or dry rot had weakened the wood. If the nail slid in easily, it was a bad sign. A board along the side of the barn could easily be replaced, but if one of the beams failed, the whole building could collapse. From where Joshua stood at the foot of the ladder, he couldn't see what his brother was discovering at the top.

"Looks *gut*," Daniel said as he came down the ladder at the same speed he would have walked up the lane.

His younger brother was finally filling out after spending the past five or six years looking like a black-haired scarecrow, disconnected joints sticking out in every direction. His shoulders were no longer too wide, and his feet and hands seemed the right size. The gaze from his bright blue eyes was steady. He and his twin Micah looked identical except for the cleft in Daniel's chin, something Daniel hated and was looking forward to hiding when he grew a beard after he married.

"No dry rot?" Joshua asked.

He shook his head. "In spite of how it looks, the barn was kept up well for many years. Any damage is recent, say the past five years or so, and it's only on the surface." He dropped the nail into a pocket of his well-worn tool belt. "But if the barn doesn't get some maintenance soon, it'll tumble in on itself."

"I know at least that much about construction, brother *boppli*." Joshua smiled, knowing how the term annoyed Daniel, who had been born more than a half hour after his twin.

"Are you sure your ancient mind can hold so much information?" his brother shot back.

Laughing with Daniel erased the rest of the tension he'd been feeling since he decided to bring Rebekah and the *kinder* to Lloyd's farm. Much of it had eased when she'd told him she would like to visit the buggy shop. Her effort to learn more about his life showed she wanted their marriage to have a chance, too.

His relief at hearing that revealed how uncertain he'd been about her expectations from their marriage. *Maybe you haven't given her a chance before today to tell you that she wanted to visit*, scolded the little voice from his conscience. He couldn't expect her to be candid when he withheld himself from her. At first he hadn't wanted to mention Tildie, because he hadn't wanted Rebekah to think he was comparing her housekeeping and interactions with the *kinder* to how his first wife would have handled them. Again he regretted not taking more time to talk before they spoke their vows. If they'd had more discussions then, the situation might be easier now.

"So how long to fix up the place?" Joshua asked.

"At least a month to do the basics, including the painting. That's assuming I can get *gut* helpers. It's not easy this time of year when everyone's so busy." He rubbed the cleft in his chin and arched his brows. "If the barn burned, everyone would be here even sooner."

"I'm hoping you aren't suggesting burning it down so we can have a barn raising."

Daniel laughed. "I never thought I'd hear my big brother, the volunteer fireman, make such a comment."

"I wanted to make sure *you* didn't." He clapped his brother on the shoulder, then looked around again. "Just a month to repair and paint? That's faster than I'd guessed."

"That's assuming I can get plenty of help. I may be able to get it done even more quickly if you're willing to hire a few of my *Englisch* coworkers."

Now Joshua was surprised. "Why wouldn't I?"

"*Englischers* think we Amish are the most skilled construction workers. I wasn't sure what you thought."

"I think I want this job done quickly and well."

"*Gut.* There are a couple of *Englisch* guys I work with who can run circles around me with a hammer and nails. I can ask them if they'd like some extra work."

He knew his brother was being modest, because Daniel's skills had an excellent reputation. "Sounds like a plan."

"I'm pretty sure one will, because he's been talking about his wife wanting him to take the family on a trip to Florida."

"How much are you planning to charge me?" Joshua asked with mock horror.

"Don't worry. It'll be fair. Let me talk to the guys I have in mind, and I'll get back to you soon. Okay?"

"*Ja.*"

After Daniel left, Joshua wiped his brow with a soiled handkerchief and walked across the freshly mown backyard. He waved to Levi, who was now cutting the front yard. A glance at the garden told him Debbie and Sammy had finished there. The back door was open, so he headed toward it to find out how much longer Rebekah needed at the house.

He jumped back as a large box was carried out of the kitchen. Only when it had passed did he realize his oldest was toting it. He watched, puzzled, as Timothy set it in the wagon beside a pair of ladder-back chairs.

"What's in the box?" Joshua asked.

"Some stuff Rebekah wants to take home with us."

He nodded, even though he was curious what was in the box. Her clothing and the boy's as well as the clothing she'd prepared for the *boppli* were already at his house. He'd brought Sammy's toys and several of her quilts the first week after they were married.

"I hope the rest will fit," his son said.

"Depends on how much else there is," Joshua replied as his mind whirled.

Rebekah hadn't said anything to him about bringing any of her furniture to his house. Tildie had remarked often what a comfortable home it was. Didn't Rebekah have everything she needed?

What if their situations were reversed? There were some items he'd want to bring with him into her house. His buggy supply catalogues, the lamp that was the perfect height when he was reading, his favorite pillow and the quilt *Grossmammi* Stoltzfus had made for him, some of Tildie's rag rugs…and, most important, the family Bible.

"I don't know what else she's planning to bring," Timothy said. "She's in the house. You can ask her while I pack the rest of the canned food."

"I will."

As his son headed toward a bulkhead door and vanished down the stairs to the cellar, Joshua went to the kitchen door. The last time he'd come this way was to ask Rebekah to marry him.

He entered the kitchen. "Do you intend on bringing much more...?" His voice faded as he glanced around in disbelief. The kitchen cabinets looked abandoned because the stove and refrigerator were gone. The table where he'd sat while he discussed marriage with Rebekah had vanished, too. He looked through to the living room. Except for the sewing machine, the other room was empty, too. He frowned. Timothy had brought out only a box and the two chairs. Where was everything else?

He heard footfalls upstairs. He climbed the steps two at a time and followed the sound of muffled voices past a bathroom. Glancing into a room on the other side of the hall, he guessed it'd been a bedroom. It was empty except for a carved blanket chest. The top was open, and a tumbling-blocks quilt in shades of green, black and white was draped over the edge.

He kept going and looked into the other bedroom. Rebekah stood in the middle of it, her hands pressed to her mouth as if trying to hold in a cry. Debbie and Sammy stood on either side of her, for once silent.

Catching his daughter's eyes, Joshua motioned with his head for Debbie to leave. She obeyed, bringing Sammy with her. He smiled at her and patted her shoulder.

"Rebekah's sad," she whispered before she led the little boy down the stairs.

No, he thought as he walked into the room. Rebekah

wasn't sad. She was furious. Every inch of her bristled with anger.

"Where is your furniture?" he asked when she didn't acknowledge him.

"Gone," she said, slowly lowering her hands.

"Gone?" He knew he sounded silly repeating what she'd said, but he was stunned to find another room stripped of everything including the dark green shades. "We need to let the bishop know you've been robbed. He can inform your neighbors and the police."

She put a hand on his arm, halting him. His astonishment that she'd purposely touched him instead of shying away eclipsed his shock with the stripped house.

"There's no need to alert the bishop. The day of our wedding I told my *mamm* to let Lloyd's family know they were welcome to take anything they could use." She drew in a deep breath and gave him a weak smile. "I guess they needed a lot."

"They took all the furniture?"

"Except my sewing machine, a pair of wooden chairs that belonged to my *aenti* and the blanket chest my *grossdawdi* built for me when I was twelve." She struggled to hold back the tears shining in her eyes. "I put the linens they left in the box Timothy's already taken out."

He thought about the box in the wagon. It wasn't very large. "What about your cradle? Where is it?"

"I don't have a cradle. Sammy slept in a drawer for a few months after he was born, and then I devised a pallet for him until he was big enough to sleep in a regular bed."

Joshua frowned. He recalled very clearly Lloyd bragging about the beautiful, handmade cradle he had ordered from a woodworker in Ephrata. His friend apologized for his boasting, saying he was excited to be able to give such a fine gift to his wife. He'd even stopped by to show it off. Joshua remembered it well because it'd been his and Tildie's wedding anniversary, and Joshua had had to push aside his grief to try to share his friend's excitement. Lloyd had said he planned to present it to Rebekah the following week.

But he hadn't. What had happened to the beautiful cradle? Uneasiness was an icy river running through him. For some reason, Lloyd must have needed to sell the cradle before he gave it to Rebekah. Joshua tried to guess what would have been more important to his friend than providing for his wife and *kind*.

Chapter Nine

Rebekah drew back on Dolly's reins to slow the buggy as it neared the parking lot where a sign painted with Stoltzfus Family Shops was set prominently to one side. The long, low red clapboard building held the local grocery store, which was owned by her brother-in-law, Amos, as well as the other shops where the brothers worked. The scent of hot metal came from Isaiah's smithy behind the main building, a *gut* sign because Isaiah was again working after taking time off in the wake of his wife's death.

Joshua's brother was moving forward with his life, and she must do the same. The sight of the empty rooms at the house in Bird-in-Hand had been shocking, but also felt like closing the pages of a book. An ending. She was beginning a new story with Joshua's family in Paradise Springs. Everything that had been part of that life was gone, except for the farm. She was grateful she wouldn't have to make a decision about it now.

A few cars and a trio of buggies were parked in front of the grocery store. When she halted her buggy, she heard the clip-clop of several horses. An *Englisch* man came around the end of the building leading four horses. He nodded toward her as he walked toward a horse trailer at the far end of the parking lot.

She watched him load the horses in with the ease of practice. It was amusing to think of horses riding.

"Sit here? No go?" Sammy asked when she didn't move to get out of the buggy.

Rebekah looked at her son, who held a bag of cookies he'd brought from the house. He wanted to see the buggy shop, too. The other *kinder*, who'd been to the shop often, were helping *Grossmammi* Wanda and *Aenti* Esther prepare pots of flowering plants to sell at the end of the farm lane. Passersby stopped and bought them along with the cheeses Joshua's brother Ezra made.

"Let's go." She smiled at his excitement. It was infectious. She was eager to see where Joshua spent so many hours each day.

Still holding the bag, Sammy grabbed her hand as soon as she came around the buggy and swung him down. She winced when the motion she'd done so often sent a streak of pain across her back. A warning, she knew, to be careful. The ache subsided into a dull throbbing that matched her steps across the asphalt parking lot and up onto the concrete sidewalk in front of Joshua's shop.

Stoltzfus Buggy Shop.

The small sign was in one corner of the window beside the door next to another one announcing the shop was open. The hours were listed on the door, but Joshua was willing to come in early or stay late to help a customer.

As she opened the door, a bell chimed overhead and a buzzer echoed beyond an arch at the far end of the large room. It must lead into another space, but a partially closed door kept her from seeing. A half wall was a few paces from the doorway. On the other side were partially built buggies, spare parts and several hulking machines. The only one she recognized was a sewing machine with a table wider and longer than her own. She guessed it was for sewing upholstery for the buggies.

"What are you doing here?"

Rebekah recoiled from the deep voice coming out of a small room to the right, then realized it belonged to Timothy. She hadn't realized before how much he sounded like a grown man. There wasn't any anger on his face, even though his voice had been sharp. Maybe it was as simple as he always sounded annoyed.

"Cookies!" Sammy announced, oblivious to the teenager's tone. Running to the half wall, he held up the bag. "Yummy cookies."

"*Danki*, little man." Timothy gave a gentle tug on Sammy's hair.

Her son smiled as if Timothy was the greatest person in the world. He offered the bag again to the teenager. Timothy took it, unrolled the top and held it out so Sammy could select a cookie.

Biting her lower lip, Rebekah stayed silent. It was such a sweet moment, and she didn't want to do anything to shatter it.

The older boy looked over Sammy's head. "*Danki*, Rebekah."

"The cookies are—"

"No, I mean *danki* for telling *Daed* I don't want to build buggies. We had a long talk about it this morning."

"You did?"

"*Ja*. He suggested I try working a while with each of my *onkels* and see if I want to learn a craft from one of them." He grinned. "So, starting next week, I'll work here half the day and with *Onkel* Jeremiah the other half. If making furniture doesn't interest me, and I'm not sure it will, I can apprentice with a different *onkel*. I think I'll like working at *Onkel* Isaiah's smithy or at the grocery store best."

"What a *gut* idea!"

"It was mine. *Daed* actually listened when I suggested it."

"Your *daed* is always willing to listen to a well-thought-out idea shared with him in a calm tone."

He rolled his eyes, making Sammy giggle. "Okay, Rebekah. I get the message. Lower volume, more thought."

She laughed and patted his shoulder, pleased he allowed it. "Timothy Stoltzfus, that sounds like something a grown man would say."

He started to roll his eyes again, but halted when Joshua came around the door in the arch. "Who's at the door, Timothy?" He wiped his hands on an oily cloth as he walked toward the half wall. A smile brightened his face. "Rebekah, you should have told me you were planning to come this afternoon. I would have cleaned up some of this mess."

"It looks fine," she replied. "We decided you needed some cookies."

"Cookies!" Sammy pointed to the bag Timothy held.

"More like crumbs." Timothy shook the bag so they could hear the broken cookie pieces in it. "But they taste *gut*, don't they, Sammy?"

"Gut! Gut! Gut!" The toddler danced around in a circle.

Joshua chuckled. "Why don't you take Sammy over to *Onkel* Amos's store, Timothy, and buy each of you something cool to enjoy with your cookie bits? Tell him I'll stop by later to pay for it."

"I've got money." Timothy squared his shoulders, trying to look taller. "Brad Granger paid me for helping him clean out his garage a couple of weeks ago. C'mon, little man. Let's see what *Onkel* Amos has that's yummy."

Sammy gave him his hand and went out the door. He waved back through the glass.

"What a surprise!" Joshua ran his fingers through his beard as he stared after the boys until they walked out of view. "I didn't expect him to spend his hard-earned money. He's been saving up for something, though he hasn't said what."

"Timothy has a *gut* heart," she said.

"Which he hides most of the time."

"All the more reason to be appreciative when he reveals it."

"True." He opened the swinging door in the half wall and motioned for her to come in. "What would you like to see first?"

"Everything!" She laughed as she lifted off her bonnet and put it on a nearby table. Smoothing her hair back toward her *kapp*, she said, "Now I sound like Sammy when he's excited. Can you show me what you're working on?"

He led the way past the machines, identifying each one by what it did. All were powered by air compression. Most were for working with metal when he built buggy wheels or put together the structure for the main part of the buggy. As she'd guessed, the sewing machine was used for making the seat upholstery. Tools hung from pegboard along one long wall. Hammers of every size as well as screwdrivers and wrenches. Those were the tools she recognized. Others she'd never seen before. She wanted to ask what they were used for, but her attention was caught by the fancy vehicle on the other side of the arch.

The grand carriage was parked in front of wide double doors. It was much larger than their family buggy and painted a pristine white. Open, with its top folded down at the back, it had two sets of seats that faced each other behind a raised seat, which had been painted a lustrous black at the front. The curved side wall dipped down toward a single step so someone could enter the carriage. The tufted seats were upholstered in bright red velvet. Large white wheels were topped by a curved piece of metal so no mud or stones from the road could strike the occupants. Narrow rubber tires edged the wheels.

"This is my current project," Joshua said as he placed one hand on the side of the carriage.

"What is it?"

"Mr. Carpenter, the *Englischer* who asked me to restore it, told me it's called a vis-à-vis. It's a French phrase that means the passengers face each other."

"It's really fancy and really fanciful, like something a princess would ride in." She stroked the red velvet. "Does he drive it?"

"Apparently he intends to use it on his daughter's wedding day. He tells me he has two matched bay horses to pull it to the church."

She arched her brows, and he chuckled. After walking to the body of a plain gray buggy, she bent to look inside it. "Are you repairing this, too?"

"No. I'm building it for a family near New Holland. I start with a wood base, then make the frame out of metal. Once it's secure, boards enclose it and the body is painted. Next I need to add wiring for lights and put in the dashboard Jeremiah is making." He glanced at a wall calendar from the bank in Paradise Springs. The squares were filled with notations in a multitude of colored inks. She guessed it was Joshua's schedule for each vehicle he was working on when he added, "He's supposed to have the dash to me soon."

She listened, fascinated, while he described making and fitting the wheels to a vehicle, as well as building the shafts to harness the horse to it. The interior would be completed to the new owner's specifications. He pointed to a list of options tacked on the wall. She was amazed to see almost two dozen items until she realized it was for many different kinds of vehicles. A young man wanted a certain style of seat in his courting buggy, while a family might need an extra bench seat or choose to have a pickup-style bed for moving bulky items.

"I never guessed it took so many different steps to make a buggy," she said when he finished the tour. "They're far more complicated than I'd guessed."

"It's our goal to let our customers think their buggies are simple so they won't need much maintenance to keep them going. That's why I want each buggy we make to be the best we can do."

"That sounds like pride, Joshua Stoltzfus," she teased.

"It does." He patted the unfinished buggy. "But what

if I say I'm glad God gave me the skill to put a *gut* buggy together?"

"Better."

"*Gut*. Let me show you the sewing machine. I think you'll find it interesting."

Rebekah took a single step to follow him, then paused as she pressed her hands to her lower back. The faint throb had erupted into an agonizing ache when she moved.

Did she groan? She wasn't sure, but Joshua rushed to her. He put his arm around her shoulders, urging her to lean on him. Her cheek rested on his chest while he guided her to a chair by the half wall, and she felt the smooth, strong motion of his muscles.

"Are you okay?" His warm breath sifted along her neck, making her *kapp* strings flutter…and her heart, as well.

"*Ja*. I strained my back while lifting Sammy out of the carriage. He's getting bigger, and so am I." She tried to laugh, but halted when another pang ricocheted up her spine. "I won't make that mistake again."

"Take Debbie with you when you're going out with Sammy. She'll be glad to help."

"I know." She glanced up at him. "She's helping your *mamm* and Esther today. She was hoping her friend, Mandy, would come over, too."

"But she would be happy to help you."

"I know. You have raised a very sweet daughter."

Her words touched him, she saw. *Hochmut* wasn't a part of the Amish way, but he knew how blessed he was that his *kinder* had stayed strong after the death of their *mamm*.

With his hand at the center of her back, he steered

her toward the half wall, where she could sit while they waited for Timothy and Sammy to return. It was a simple motion she'd seen him use with the *kinder*, but his light caress sent a powerful quiver along her. Even when he didn't touch her, she was deeply aware of him. To have his fingers brushing her waist threatened to demolish the wall she had built around her heart to keep any man from ever touching it.

When she lowered herself to the chair, he knelt beside her. He took her hand between his much broader ones. Worry etched deep threads in his brow. Before she could halt them, her fingers stroked his forehead to ease those lines. They slipped down his smooth cheek, edging his soft but wiry beard.

His brown eyes, as liquid and warm as melted chocolate, were filled with pleasure at her caress and questions about what she intended it to mean. How could she explain when she didn't know herself?

Drawing her hands away, she clasped them atop her full belly. The motion seemed to free them from the powerful connection between them. Or so she thought until he put his hand over hers, and the *boppli* kicked hard enough that he must have felt it, too. A loving glow filled his eyes exactly like when he looked at his own *kinder*.

"A strong one," he murmured.

"The *boppli* doesn't like to be ignored."

A slow smile curved his lips and sparkled in his eyes. "Maybe it's giving us fair warning to be prepared for when it's born."

She laughed. "I would prefer to think it's getting its antics out of the way so it'll be a *gut boppli*."

"You sound as if you're feeling better." His voice remained low and tender.

"I am. Sitting helps."

"*Gut.* Tomorrow I'll stop at the clinic and make an appointment for you. I'll ask them to see you as soon as possible."

"I told you, Joshua, the back pain was nothing but me being foolish."

He shook his head. "That may be so, but you need to see a midwife. You've been here more than a month, and if I remember right, you should be having appointments with her frequently at this point."

"I should." She resisted stroking his face again. "*Danki*, Joshua. I appreciate your kindness more than words can express."

He opened his mouth to reply, but whatever he intended to say went unspoken because the door opened and the boys rushed in. As Timothy launched into an explanation of how long Sammy had taken to select something to drink and how the little boy had delighted the other customers with his comments, Joshua stood and pretended to admire the sweet cider Sammy had chosen.

She watched and smiled and complimented her son on his choice, but her eyes kept shifting toward Joshua. He was watching her, too. Something huge had changed between them. Something that could not go back to the way it had been.

Joshua greeted his family as he came into the kitchen the next evening. He glanced first at Rebekah, but she was, as she'd assured him at breakfast, recovered from the muscle strain that had sent waves of pain across her face at the buggy shop.

Walking to the stove where Rebekah was adding butter to peas fresh from the garden, he asked, "How are you doing today?"

"Fine." She smiled at him, and his insides bounced like a *kind* on a trampoline.

"I made an appointment for you at the clinic." He held out the card he'd been given.

"Danki." She took the card and slipped it into a pocket in her black apron. "Why don't you sit? Dinner is almost ready."

"And I'm in your way?"

He heard Debbie giggle by the sink as Rebekah nodded. Walking back to the table, he lifted Sammy into the high chair set between his chair and Rebekah's. His gaze slipped to the far end of the table where the chairs Rebekah had brought from Bird-in-Hand awaited guests. It was odd to have the extra chairs by the table, but he knew they would be useful when company came.

He still wasn't accustomed to seeing her sewing machine by the largest window in the living room or having Tildie's blanket chest at the foot of Debbie's bed. Tildie's old sewing machine was stored in the attic, waiting for someone who could use it. He'd planned on giving his daughter the chest when she married, not so soon.

His sons came in freshly washed and making no secret of how hungry they were. Rebekah put the peas and thick, smoky slices of ham in the middle of the table. Debbie filled their glasses from a pitcher of ice water before getting warm biscuits from the oven.

Another feast! Joshua patted his stomach when it growled and everyone laughed. As soon as Rebekah was sitting beside the high chair and Debbie across from her brothers, he bowed his head for grace. He had so much to be thankful for: his family, the food and how God had brought Rebekah into his life. Grateful his prayer was silent because he could speak directly from his heart, he cleared his throat and looked up when Sammy moved impatiently beside him.

The conversation was easy and as plentiful as the food. When Joshua reached for another biscuit, a strange sound erupted from beneath the table. A dull thud. He looked at his glass. The water inside was fluttering.

"What was that?" Debbie asked, her eyes round and wide.

The *kinder* as well as Rebekah looked at him in bafflement. He wished he had an answer, but he didn't.

"Maybe it was an earthquake." Levi nearly bounced off his chair with excitement. "*Aenti* Esther taught us about them last year, and I read a book from the school library about the big ones in California. Maybe we're having one, too."

"Unlikely," Joshua said. "There aren't many earthquakes in Pennsylvania."

"Oh." His son looked disappointed.

"Then what was that sound?" asked Timothy. "Why did the table shake?"

"I don't know."

Rebekah shrugged her shoulders when Joshua glanced at her again. "I don't have any idea, either."

"Whatever it was is over," he said. "Eat up. If—"

A louder thump sounded. The table vibrated hard enough so the silverware bounced. Faces around the table paled.

Joshua looked down. This time, he'd felt whatever it was hitting the floor under his feet. No, not the floor.

Something had struck the cellar's ceiling…right below the kitchen table. Right where the fuel lines came into the house from the propane tank in the backyard.

He jumped to his feet. "Rebekah, take the *kinder* outside. Now!"

"You should come, too." Her face had lost all color. "Timothy, go next door and call 911."

"Let me do a quick check before you make that call." He locked eyes with his oldest. "Be ready to run to the Grangers." He crossed the kitchen in a trio of quick steps.

"Joshua?"

He looked back to see Rebekah picking up Sammy who held a piece of bread in one hand and a slice of ham in the other. "What?"

"Be careful." Her intense gaze seconded her soft words. She'd lost one husband, and she didn't want to lose another.

For a second he was warmed by that thought and considered heading out with the rest of the family, because he didn't want to be separated from a single one of them. It would mean another of the volunteer firemen having to go into the cellar to find out what was happening. He couldn't ask another man to do what he wouldn't.

Throwing open the cellar door while his family hurried out of the kitchen, he instinctively ducked when something exploded not far from the bottom of the steps. He sniffed, but didn't smell any gas. If it wasn't a fuel leak, what was blowing up?

He took one cautious step, then another. Groping along a shelf, he pulled out the flashlight he left there for emergencies. He took another deep breath to assure himself there wasn't a gas leak. Even the small spark created by the switch on the flashlight could set off a huge explosion if the cellar was filled with propane.

The air smelled sweet. No hint of the rotten odor added to propane to alert them to danger.

Even so, he held his breath as he turned on the flashlight. Nothing erupted. He swept the cellar with light. Everything looked as it should. He took a step. When something cracked beneath his boot, he aimed the light at the floor. Shards of glass were scattered across it.

He whirled when he heard footsteps overhead. Who was in the house? He saw Rebekah at the top of the stairs. "What are you doing? I told you to get out."

"Timothy opened some of the cellar windows from the outside, and he didn't smell any gas."

"I don't, either. I don't know what exploded. I—"

He put his arms over his head as a detonation came from his left. Something wet struck him. His skin was sliced by shattered glass.

"Joshua!" Rebekah shouted.

"Daed!" That was Timothy.

"Daedi!" The younger *kinder* yelled at the same time.

Raising his head and lowering his arms, he grimaced as liquid dripped from him. Some of it was blood, he realized when a drop splattered on his boot. Above him on the stairs, Rebekah and the *kinder* wore identical expressions of dismay.

He shook the fluid off him. Or tried to. It was sticky. He sniffed his lacerated forearm. "Root beer."

Glancing at the shelves where the canned food was stacked, he saw four more bottles of root beer. He grabbed them and stuffed them beneath a wooden crate. Just in time because another exploded, making the crate rise an inch from the floor.

"No," he heard Rebekah say. "You can't go down there until you put on shoes."

Within minutes, his sons had joined him and Rebekah in the cellar. Sammy stayed with Debbie at the top of the stairs, because the little boy was too young to help clean up glass. After he reassured them he was fine other than being covered with root beer from head to foot, Joshua asked Timothy to bring water from the spring at the back corner of the cellar. They needed to wash the concrete floor before ants discovered the spilled soda. When another bottle erupted beneath the crate, everyone jumped even though they'd known it could happen.

"I didn't realize there was any root beer left," Joshua said as he swept water and glass toward the center of the floor where Timothy scooped it up and put it in the bag Levi held. "I wonder why it exploded tonight."

"It's my fault, *Daedi.*" Levi stared down at his sneakers.

"Your fault? How?"

"I moved the bottles." He looked up quickly, then at his feet again. "Rebekah asked Debbie and me to help sort out what was down here. I found the bottles and hid them behind the canned peaches."

"So you didn't have to share them? Levi, that isn't like you."

Rebekah put a hand on Joshua's arm, startling him. When he turned to her, she shook her head and gave him a gentle smile. He realized her thoughts were on his son, not on him. As he replayed his words in his mind, he knew he had spoken too harshly.

Levi was a *gut* boy, but no boy was perfect. If one who loved root beer tried to hide a few old bottles to enjoy later by himself, he should be reminded sharing something special was the best way.

"I won't do it again, *Daed*." Levi was near tears.

He clasped his younger son's shoulder. "I know you won't. Are there any more bottles back there?"

"Let me check." Timothy stepped toward the shelves. "You need to get those cuts looked at, *Daed*."

"He's right," Rebekah said gently. "Levi can finish cleaning up this mess while I tend to your injuries."

He nodded when he realized this was her way of ensuring his son wouldn't forget the bad decision he had made. Handing the broom to Levi, he said, "I know you will do a *gut* job, son."

The boy sniffed back tears, but said, "I will, *Daed*."

Joshua walked up the stairs after Rebekah. When she wobbled, he put his hand at her back to steady her. She didn't pull away. His steps were light as he went into the kitchen. Timothy being helpful, Levi admitting to the truth right away…and Rebekah not shrinking from his touch. Maybe they'd reached a turning point and their lives would get better. As he sat at the kitchen table so Rebekah could put salve on the many small cuts on his arms, he prayed that would be so.

Help me find a way to bring happiness into our lives. He hoped the prayer would be answered soon.

Chapter Ten

When Levi brought the buggy and Dolly out of the barn, Rebekah smiled. The boy had made every effort to be on his best behavior since the episode with the exploding root beer bottles three nights ago. Even on Sunday during the church service, he hadn't squirmed once or poked the boy beside him.

Now she thanked him for hooking up the horse. He gave her a shy smile before jogging toward the house where Debbie was washing the breakfast dishes and keeping an eye on Sammy.

The road was empty while Rebekah headed toward the village. The sunlight shimmered on the road in front of her, warning the day was going to be a hot one. Usually she looked forward to summer heat, but not while she was pregnant. Every degree higher on the thermometer added to her discomfort.

She went past the Stoltzfus Family Shops sign. The parking lot was filled as usual with cars and buggies. When the door of Joshua's shop opened and he bounded out, waving his hands, she drew back on the reins in astonishment.

"What's wrong?" she asked.

He didn't answer her question. He asked one of his own. "Where are you bound?"

"To my appointment with the midwife."

He grimaced, then looked down at his grease-stained shirt and trousers. "I forgot your appointment was today. Let's go." He put his foot on the step, then halted because she didn't slide across the seat.

"You don't need to come with me, Joshua. I know you're concerned about getting Mr. Carpenter's carriage done on time."

He shook his head, his most stubborn expression tightening his lips as he dropped back on to the ground. "I need to come with you. You are my wife. We will, God willing, be raising this *kind* together for many years to come." He put his foot on the step again and held out his hands.

She gave him the reins and moved to the left side of the buggy. She was glad her bonnet hid her face, because she wasn't sure what his reaction would be to the tears filling her eyes. She thought of the days since she'd visited the buggy shop and how solicitous he had been, making sure the *kinder* helped in the house and with Sammy so she could rest a short while each afternoon. Each kindness was a *wunderbaar* surprise she treasured, knowing how fleeting such benevolence could be. He'd welcomed her concerns about Timothy and accepted her silent chiding to be more gentle with his son after Levi had stashed the bottles of root beer in the cellar.

Am I being foolish to consider trusting again, God? The question came from the depths of her heart, bursting out of her unbidden. Only now did she recognize how desperately she longed for a real marriage.

As Joshua steered the buggy on to the road, a white van pulled up in front of Amos's store. An elderly man and woman were waiting with their bags of groceries, each of them holding an ice cream cone. The driver parked, jumped out and opened the door to let them in while he put their purchases in the back.

It was a scene Rebekah had witnessed often at the grocery store in Bird-in-Hand, but her breath caught when she noticed how the elderly man helped his wife into the van as if she were as precious and essential to him as his next breath. Every motion spoke of the love they shared, a love that required no words because it was part of them. She felt a pinch of envy as she imagined having a love like that to share.

When Joshua spoke, it unsettled her to realize his thoughts closely mirrored hers. "The Riehls were married before I was born. Even though Amos has offered to deliver groceries to their house, they insist on coming to the store. He suspects the real reason is the soft ice cream machine he put in last year."

"Ice cream *is* a *gut* reason." She smiled, letting her uncomfortable thoughts drain away. "Do you ever make ice cream with the *kinder*?"

"Our ice cream maker broke a few years ago."

"I brought one from the farm."

He flashed her a grin. "I'm surprised Levi hasn't been begging to make ice cream. The boy has a real sweet tooth."

"He's mentioned it several times, but…" She sighed. "There are only so many hours in each day."

"I was wondering, Rebekah, if it is wise for you to be doing so much of the housework."

She looked at him, baffled. Why wouldn't she do the house chores? It was what a wife did. Dismay twisted in her middle. Had she failed to keep the house or make his meals or clean the laundry as well as Matilda had?

"Why?" It seemed the safest question to ask.

"I see how exhausted you are. You cook and clean for four *kinder* as well as you and me. In addition, you work in the garden every day and spend hours making and keeping our clothes in *gut* repair."

"You work as hard at the buggy shop."

"But I'm not going to have a *boppli* soon." He shot her a grin. "What do you say to getting a girl in to help before the *boppli* is born? She could do the heavier chores so you can rest?" His smile broadened. "And have time to supervise making ice cream for Levi."

"That would be *wunderbaar*." Again she had to blink back tears. They seemed to be her constant companion recently. His concern touched her heart, piercing the barriers she'd raised to protect it from being hurt over and over.

"I asked around and Sadie Gingerich may be available." He drew in the reins when they reached the main highway.

Route 30 was always busy. The buggy rocked when eighteen-wheelers roared past, but Dolly acted as if she encountered them every day. The horse stood still until given the command to go. The buggy sped across, and Rebekah grasped the seat with both hands to keep from being rocked off.

When they were driving along a quiet residential street, Joshua added, "Sadie helped my sister Ruth during her last pregnancy, and Ruth was very satisfied. You haven't spent much time with my sister, but I can tell you she's not easy to please."

"Ruth knows what her family needs, and she isn't afraid to voice her opinions."

He smiled. "That's a nice way of saying she's bossy, but she's the oldest, so she's used to looking out for us. If you want, I can contact Sadie's family. They live south of Paradise Springs, closer to Strasburg. If she can't help, she might know someone she can recommend." He glanced across the buggy. "Do you want me to check if she can come?"

"*Ja.*" She couldn't say more. The tears that had filled her eyes were now clogging her throat until she felt as if she'd swallowed a lump of uncooked bread dough.

"Are you sure?"

She realized he'd taken her terse answer as dismay instead of overwhelming relief and gratitude that he cared enough about her to hire Sadie Gingerich to help. Blinking the tears hanging on her lashes, she said, "*Ja,* I'm sure. *Danki*, Joshua."

"I'll see if she can stop by soon. If you like her—and I think you will because she's a nice girl—she can start right away." He tapped her nose. When she stared at him as if he'd lost his mind, he laughed. "Then maybe my pretty wife won't have dark circles under her eyes because she's doing too much and not getting enough sleep."

"Nice way to give your wife a compliment."

"I don't want you to grow prideful." His gaze cut into her as he added, "And that can't be easy for someone as beautiful as you."

She knew she was blushing, but she didn't care.

Lloyd had never given her a compliment. Not even when they were courting. She should pay no attention to fancy words. Yet when Joshua said something nice to her, happiness filled her, making her feel as if the sun glowed inside her.

He didn't add more as he slowed the buggy again and hit the toggle that activated the right turn signal. He pulled into an extrawide driveway and stopped by a hitching post. After jumping out, he lashed the reins to it, though Dolly would wait for them to return.

Rebekah was glad when he assisted her out of the buggy. It wasn't easy to see her feet now, especially on the narrow step. Gravel crunched beneath her feet as she walked with him toward the single-story white building that looked as if it had been a home. Dark green shutters edged the windows. A bright wreath with purple and white blossoms hung on the yellow door, and a small plaque to one side announced: Paradise Springs Birthing Clinic.

Joshua reached past her to open the door. It wasn't until she was inside that she realized she hadn't cringed away from his arm when it had edged around her. She was torn between joy and praying that she wasn't making another huge mistake. She wasn't going to think about the dark times. They had shadowed her life for too long. She was going to focus on the here and now. And the *boppli* who would be born soon.

The clinic was as cheerful and bright inside as it was on the exterior. A half dozen plastic chairs in a variety of colors edged each side of the room. Three were occupied, and none of the women were dressed plainly. They looked up and smiled as she walked past. She returned their smiles and told herself to relax.

After going to the registration desk near a closed door at the far end of the narrow room, Rebekah gave her name to the receptionist who wore large, red-rimmed glasses. The receptionist welcomed her and handed her a clipboard with forms to fill out.

Rebekah sat and concentrated on answering each question. Joshua took the chair beside her.

"Measles?" he asked when she checked a box on the long list of common diseases. "Didn't you have the shot when you were a *kind*?"

"I did, but I caught them anyhow." She chuckled. "The doctor told *Mamm* it sometimes happens that way and that I would have been much sicker if I hadn't had the shot. I couldn't imagine how, because I was pretty sick with them."

Turning the page over, she was glad the portion on health insurance had already been crossed out. That showed the clinic was accustomed to dealing with the Amish, who weren't required to purchase health insurance because their community took care of any medical bills a family couldn't pay on their own.

But how was she going to pay for the *boppli*'s birth? She couldn't expect Joshua to pay the costs. The *boppli* wasn't his. The answer came instantly: she'd have to sell the farm in Bird-in-Hand. Once the farm was gone, her haven would be, too, but what choice did she have?

Finishing the rest of the pages, she started to rise to take the completed forms to the desk.

Joshua stood and held out his hand. "Let me do that. You should sit while you can."

As she thanked him, a woman sitting on her other side leaned toward her. "You have a very considerate husband," she whispered. "I wish my husband understood like yours does how tough it is to get up and down." She laughed. "My ankles are getting as big as a house."

Taken aback, Rebekah wasn't sure how to reply. She gave the woman a smile, which seemed the perfect answer because the other woman laughed and went back to reading her book.

Joshua sat beside her again. "The receptionist said it shouldn't be long before you're called in."

"Gut." The plastic chair was uncomfortable.

A few minutes later the inner door opened. A tall woman stepped out. Her dark brown hair was swept back beneath a *kapp* that identified her as a Mennonite. The back was pleated and square rather than heart-shaped like Rebekah's. Her plain gown was worn beneath a doctor's white coat, and a stethoscope hung around her neck. She called out Rebekah's name. When Joshua stood, too, the woman asked him to wait, saying he'd be called back in a few minutes.

He nodded and took his seat. He gave Rebekah a bolstering smile as she went to the door and stepped through into a hallway that branched off past two open doors on either side.

"This way, Rebekah," the woman in the white coat said.

In spite of knowing she shouldn't, Rebekah stared at the woman who limped as she walked. A plastic brace ran from below her right knee into her black sneaker. It was held in place atop her black stockings by a wide strip of what looked like Velcro.

She recovered herself and followed the woman into a room. The midwife's warm smile was so genuine that she was instantly at ease.

"I am Elizabeth Overholt, but everyone calls me Beth Ann," said the woman before she asked Rebekah to get on the scale. She then checked Rebekah's blood pressure. Rebekah was pleased with both, and so was Beth Ann.

"Excellent," Beth Ann said and led her to a room across the hall. She motioned for Rebekah to come in. "Do you need help getting on the table?"

"I think I can manage still."

"Don't be brave. Ask for help when you need it." She kept her hand near Rebekah's elbow until Rebekah was sitting on the examination table. "Okay, I have your file from your midwife in Bird-in-Hand, so let's see what it says."

Looking around the pleasant room while Beth Ann read the file, Rebekah smiled. Childish drawings hung on the wall. She guessed one of them depicted a kitten or maybe a lamb. Something with curly, fuzzy hair. The other was of a *kind* holding a woman's hand. A small house and a huge tree were behind them, and the sun was bright yellow while a rainbow arched over the whole scene.

Booklets she recognized from when she'd been pregnant with Sammy were stacked neatly by the window. Then she had read every word, hungry for information to make sure her *boppli* was born healthy. Not one had contained any advice on how to keep her husband from damaging their *kind*.

She pushed the dreary cloud of memory away. Lloyd was gone, and Joshua hadn't raised his hand to her. Not yet.

Oh, Lord, help me to trust he's not the man Lloyd

was. I want to be able to believe he won't hurt me or the kinder.

Beth Ann looked up, and her smile vanished. "Is everything okay, Rebekah?"

"Ja." She forced a laugh that sounded brittle in her ears. "It's impossible to get comfortable at this point."

"Are you having contractions?"

She shook her head, sorry she was causing the midwife worry. But how could she be honest? She could not let Lloyd's sins become a shadow over his son as people watched to see if he had inherited his *daed*'s violent outbursts.

As she began to answer Beth Ann's questions, she told herself again, *Think about now.* Maybe if she reminded herself of that enough times, she'd make it a habit and would finally be able to leave the darkness behind her once and for all.

Joshua had been in places, but not many, where he felt less comfortable than in the waiting room with a group of *Englisch* women who looked ready to give birth at any moment. None of the magazines stacked on the tables interested him enough to page through one until he noticed a sports magazine tucked at the bottom of one pile. He drew it out and almost laughed out loud when he saw it was a year old. The cover story was on baseball, so he began to read. He glanced toward the inner door when it opened, but it was a different woman calling out the name of one of the pregnant women.

"Mr. Stoltzfus?"

At his name, he looked up and saw the midwife who wore the brace and who'd come to get Rebekah was holding the door open again.

"Will you come with me?" she asked with a smile that suggested she knew exactly how eager he was to escape the waiting room.

Joshua had a smile of his own when he entered the room where Rebekah sat on a paper-topped examination table, her feet swinging as if she were no older than Sammy. He went to stand beside her.

After the midwife introduced herself, Beth Ann pulled out a low stool and sat. She handed him a sheet of paper. Scanning it, he saw it was a to-do list for when Rebekah's contractions started, including when to call Beth Ann.

"At that point, I will contact the doctor so he'll be there if we need him," the midwife said. "As Rebekah didn't have any complications with her first pregnancy, I don't see any reason to expect any this time. God willing, of course."

He nodded. "We have been praying for God's blessing on this birth."

"Do you have any questions?" Beth Ann asked.

"Not after having been present at the birth of my three *kinder*."

"All right, *Daedi*," she said with a laugh. "You are clearly an expert."

"I know enough to call for you to come."

That Rebekah didn't correct Beth Ann's assumption he was the *boppli*'s *daed* pleased him for a reason he couldn't decipher. He didn't want to. He wanted to enjoy the *gut* news that Rebekah and the *boppli* were doing well.

He assisted Rebekah from the table, thanked the midwife and nodded when she instructed them to make another appointment for two weeks from today. He took the small bag Rebekah held. She told him it contained vitamins. While she made an appointment, he went to get his straw hat and her bonnet from the rack by the door.

Cautiously he put his hand on her elbow to guide her on the steps and across the driveway to the buggy. Again he was relieved when she didn't tug away or flinch.

She was quiet as he started the drive toward home. He guessed she was exhausted. Crossing the highway took more than twice as long this time because the traffic was even heavier. When a tourist pointed a camera at the buggy, he leaned into the shadows so his face wouldn't be visible in the photograph. Most visitors understood the Amish didn't want to have their picture taken, but a few didn't care.

Once they crossed Route 30 and drove out of the village, no more cars zipped past them. He waved to an *Englischer* who was driving a tractor. He recognized the man from the charity mud sale at his *mamm's* house in the spring. From what he'd heard, the *Englischer* was planning to run an organic vegetable farm. Joshua appreciated the man's determination to practice *gut* husbandry.

After stopping to collect the mail, Joshua drove up the driveway. He glanced at Rebekah when she stirred. Had she fallen asleep? He didn't want to embarrass her by asking.

"*Danki* for taking me to my appointment today," she said.

"You are my wife, and that *boppli* will be growing up in my house." He felt her tense, but her shoulders became softer next to his as he added, "In our house. I'm sorry I didn't say that first."

"You don't have to apologize. That house has been yours for years. You can't expect to change old habits overnight." She flashed him a smile. "I know I haven't been able to change mine, though I'm trying to."

Was she talking about how she flinched from him? If so, he hoped her words meant she was making an effort to accept him being close to her. Because, he realized, he wanted to be close to her. The sound of her laughter, the twinkle in her eyes when she looked as mischievous as Sammy, the gentleness she used with the *kinder*, the ruddy warmth of her hair…each of these and more drew him to her.

He assisted her out of the buggy, teasing her because she was getting almost too wide for the narrow door. He started to suggest that he grill some hamburgers for their supper tonight so she could rest, but halted when he saw Sammy running toward them with Debbie on his heels. The *kinder* were barefoot, and their clothes were spotted with water above the wet hems.

"*Daedi*, come see!" yelled Sammy. "Froggie!"

Joshua couldn't move as Lloyd's son called him *Daedi* again as he tugged on Joshua's hand. This was a complication he hadn't seen coming. What should he do?

He didn't look in Rebekah's direction, fearing he would see pain and grief on her face when her late husband's son called another man *Daedi*. An apology burned on his tongue, but what could he say even if he let the words out? He wouldn't apologize for loving the *kind*, especially when Sammy reminded him of his own boys at that age. Curious and excited over the most mundane things, filled with joy and eager to share his happiness with everyone around him. Even something as commonplace as a frog was a reason for celebrating.

"Daedi!" Sammy's voice tore him away from his musing. "Quick! Froggie jumping."

"We're coming," Joshua said. "Go ahead. We'll be right behind you." As the *kinder* raced toward the stream beyond the barn, he began, "Rebekah…" Again words failed him.

She gave him the same gentle smile he'd seen her offer the *kinder* when they were distressed. It eased the tightness in his gut.

"It's all right, Joshua. He needs a *daed*, and if you're willing to be his, that's *wunderbaar.*"

"Are you sure?"

"Ja. I think you'll be the very best *daed* he could have."

"Now, you mean." He didn't want to be compared to his best friend when Lloyd had no chance to prove he would be a *gut daed* for Sammy.

She nodded, but her gaze edged away. She was hiding something, but what? He was certain if he could answer that question, so many other puzzles would be solved, too.

Chapter Eleven

The day was beautiful, and that morning before going to the shop, Joshua and Timothy had finished stringing the new clothesline out to the maple tree. Rebekah gazed at the puffy clouds as she hung a wet sheet that flapped against her in the breeze. She saw no sign of a storm, which meant she could do another load of laundry and have it dried and folded before she needed to leave for her scheduled appointment with the midwife. She'd persuaded Joshua that she was fine to go on her own. He relented only when she reminded him how his *Englisch* client would be stopping by tomorrow to collect his fancy carriage, and Joshua wanted to check it from front to back one last time to make sure he hadn't overlooked something.

"Are you Rebekah?" A cheery voice broke into her thoughts.

She looked around the sheet and saw a woman close to her own age walking toward her. Glancing past her, she didn't see a buggy. Had the woman walked to the house?

The woman's dark brown eyes sparkled in her round

face. Rather short, she was what Rebekah's *mamm* might have described as pleasingly plump. Not over-weight, but her plain clothes didn't hide that she had softer curves than what the *Englischers* deemed ideal.

"Ja," Rebekah replied. "I'm Rebekah."

"I'm Sadie Gingerich. Your husband asked me to stop by to talk about working for you." Her gaze slipped along Rebekah. "That *boppli* is coming soon, ain't so?"

She laced her fingers over her belly. "No secret about that. Let's go inside and sit while we talk."

"Sounds *gut*," Sadie agreed, but Rebekah quickly discovered that Sadie's idea of a conversation was doing most of the talking herself.

They'd no sooner sat at the kitchen table than Debbie and Sammy came from the living room where they'd been playing a game. Rebekah was pleased to see how quickly Sammy hoisted himself into Sadie's lap while she explained what work she did for a family before and after a *boppli* arrived.

Even though she didn't get a chance to ask many questions, Rebekah decided Sadie would be a great temporary addition to their household. Sadie, though she was unmarried and had no *kinder* of her own, had helped raise her eleven younger siblings. She'd started hiring out after her *daed* died and clearly loved the work she did. Whenever she spoke with Debbie or Sammy, her smile broadened, and she soon had them giggling.

"When can you start?" Rebekah asked.

"I have another week at the Millers' in the village, but I can begin after that if that works for you." She bounced a delighted Sammy on her leg as if he were riding a horse.

"That would be *wunderbaar*. Oh…" She abruptly realized they didn't have an extra bedroom for Sadie.

When she explained that, Sadie waved aside her concerns. "If Debbie doesn't mind, I'll share with her. I have almost a dozen sisters and brothers. Sharing with one other person will seem like luxury."

"Say *ja*, Rebekah," the little girl pleaded before turning to Sadie. "I've been praying the *boppli* is a girl because I want a sister."

"I'll be your practice sister." Sadie looked at Rebekah. "If that's okay with you."

"It sounds like a *gut* solution." She'd have to explain to Sadie eventually that Joshua had his own room upstairs, but that was a conversation she wanted to delay as long as possible. It wasn't that she was ashamed of the situation. She felt… She wasn't sure what she felt about it. She simply knew she didn't want to discuss it.

They spoke a while longer, then Sadie said she needed to return to the Millers' house. She left on a scooter like the ones the *kinder* rode to school, which explained why Rebekah hadn't heard a buggy approach.

Rebekah couldn't wait to tell Joshua that Sadie Gingerich had agreed to help. That made her smile even more as she went back outside to the clothesline. Lately, the idea of sharing events of the day and telling him funny stories about the *kinder* seemed natural. And she liked that they were becoming more and more a part of each other's lives. Their marriage wasn't a perfect love story, but it was getting better each day.

Once she'd finished hanging the rest of the laundry, Rebekah picked up the basket and went into the laundry area off the kitchen. She started the washer and dumped in detergent. Of all the conveniences they enjoyed from the solar panels on the roof, having a washer that wasn't run by a gasoline motor was her favorite. She'd despised the raucous noise and the fumes, even with an exhaust pipe stuck out a window, from the washer in Bird-in-Hand.

She went to the pile of light-colored clothes waiting to be washed. The *kinder* brought their dirty clothes to the laundry room, saving her extra trips up and down the stairs. They tried to sort them properly, but she occasionally found a dark sock in with the whites. She picked up each garment and shook it to make sure nothing hid within it.

When she lifted one of Joshua's light blue shirts to put it in the washer, a familiar odor, one she'd hoped never to smell again, swirled through her senses, stripping her happiness away as if it'd never existed. Her nose wrinkled. She knew that odor…and she hated it. The scent of alcohol. She'd smelled it too many times on Lloyd's breath and on his clothes.

Where was it coming from?

She sniffed the shirt. No, not from that. Dropping it into the water filling the tub, she held another piece of clothing to her nose, then another and another, and drew in a deep breath with each one. She identified the musty scent of sweat and the tangy sauce from the casserole she'd made two nights ago. The unmistakable scent of horse and another of the grease Joshua used at the buggy shop. Green and earthy aromas from the knees of the pants Levi had been wearing when he helped her weed the garden and harvest the cabbage and green beans.

But the scent of liquor was gone. Had she actually smelled it? Maybe the combination of laundry detergent and heat in the laundry room had created the odor she dreaded. After all, though she'd watched carefully, she'd never heard Joshua slur his words or seen him unsteady on his feet. He never struck her or the *kinder*.

Was the smell only her imagination? It must have been.

But what if it wasn't?

She leaned forward against the washer and whispered, "Help me, God! Help us all."

The rest of the day passed in a blur. Rebekah couldn't help taking a deep breath every few minutes. The odor of alcohol, if it'd existed at all, had vanished. It was impossible to forget the stab of fear in the laundry room. Even at her appointment with Beth Ann, she'd struggled to focus on the midwife's questions and suggestions. She'd managed little more than a faint smile when Beth Ann had congratulated her on hiring Sadie Gingerich.

The comment reminded her that Joshua was paying the expenses for Lloyd's *kind*. She shied away from the idea of selling the farm. Even after the house had been stripped clean by Lloyd's relatives, there was enough farm machinery to sell to cover the costs of the delivery and Sadie's help. How could she hold on to the farm when Joshua worked so hard to provide for the family?

By the time she returned home, her head was pounding. She must have looked as bad as she felt, because Debbie urged her to rest. She hesitated until the little girl reminded her that Joshua had volunteered to bring home pizza to celebrate finishing the work on the carriage.

Sleep eluded her. The *boppli* seemed to have acquired a love for step dancing, and her thoughts were strident. Each time she tried to divert them by praying or thinking of something else, she was drawn right back into the morass.

Usually she loved having store-bought pizza with its multitude of toppings, but she could barely tolerate the smell. She picked at a single piece while the rest of the family enjoyed the treat and the celebration. Somehow she managed to put on a *gut* front, because neither the *kinder* nor Joshua asked if something was bothering her. In fact, the whole family seemed giddy with happiness.

She wanted to feel that way, too. Was she going to allow a single scent, which might not even have been there, ruin her whole day? Again she prayed for God's help, adding a silent apology for spiraling into the terror that had stalked her during her first marriage.

The feeling of a worthless weight being lifted from her shoulders brought back her smile...and her appetite. Rebekah finished the slice of pizza and then had two more. She smiled when Timothy and Debbie began to tease Levi about a girl he'd been seen talking to several times during the past week while working with *Onkel* Daniel. As he turned the tables and jested with his sister about fleeing from the chicken coop and a particularly mean hen that had chased her halfway to the house, Rebekah joined in with the laughter.

After they finished their treat, Joshua volunteered his and the boys' help to clean up the kitchen. She started to protest, but he insisted. Grateful, she went with the younger *kinder* into the living room and sat next to the sewing basket where her hand mending was piled. No matter how often she worked on it, the stack never seemed to get smaller. She took the topmost item, a pair of Levi's trousers that needed to have the hems lowered…again! The boy was sprouting up faster than the corn in the fields.

It didn't take Joshua and his sons long to redd up the kitchen and join them. The boys sat on the floor, and she assumed Joshua would read to them as he did each evening.

"I have something else for our celebration tonight." He smiled at Rebekah. "A birthday gift."

"Joshua, it's not my birthday," she replied.

"Who said it was for you?"

She stared after him as he walked out the door. Hearing a muffled giggle from Debbie, she saw the little girl had her hands clamped over her mouth. Her eyes twinkled with merriment. Levi wouldn't meet Rebekah's gaze and Timothy, for once, was grinning broadly. Only Sammy, playing with his blocks on the braided rug, seemed oblivious.

What were they up to?

Her answer came when Joshua returned to the living room. He placed a cradle by her chair.

She gasped when she ran her fingers along the cradle's hood. The wood was as smooth as a rose petal, and it had been polished to highlight the grain. Maple, she guessed, because it had been finished to a soft honey shade. Not a single nail head was visible, and she saw dovetail joints at the corners. Her eyes widened when she realized it had been built with pegs. Only an extremely skilled woodworker could have finished the cradle using such old-fashioned techniques.

"What do you think?" Joshua asked, squatting on the other side of the cradle. "As a birthday gift for the *boppli*? Like I said, it isn't for *your* birthday." He chuckled and the *kinder* joined in.

Rebekah was speechless at the magnificent gift and even more so that Joshua had gotten it for her. A warmth built within her, melting the ice clamped on to her heart.

She whispered the only word she could manage, *"Danki."*

"I hope you like it. Jeremiah built it."

"It's beautiful."

"He does *gut* work."

She stared at the cradle and knew that *gut* was a feeble description of the lovely piece. Jeremiah must have spent hours sanding the wood and staining it and polishing it until the grain was gloriously displayed. She couldn't imagine the amount of time it had taken to cut the corners to fit together so smoothly.

"Do you like it?" Debbie asked, inching across the floor to run her fingers along the wood.

Before she could answer, Levi began a story about how Joshua had asked them to keep the secret until the cradle was finished. Even Timothy added to the tale.

Looking at their animated faces, she smiled at her family.

Her family.

Sometime in the past weeks, this house had become home and these *kinder* as much a part of her life as Sammy. And Joshua? She couldn't imagine her days without him being a part of them. His gentle teasing, his solicitude, his joy when Sammy called him *Daedi*.

Because Sammy loved him.

And, she realized with a start, she wanted to let herself fall in love with him, too. Really in love, not this make-believe marriage. She wished they could share a love not overshadowed by fear and uncertainty.

"It's lovely," Rebekah said to Debbie, giving the girl a hug. "*Danki* for letting this be a surprise."

"*Daedi* said you didn't have a cradle for Sammy, and we wanted you to have one for my little sister." She winked as Levi insisted, as Debbie had hoped he would in response to her teasing, that the *boppli* was a boy.

Joshua glanced at his *kinder*, then said, "I'm glad you like it, Rebekah. I was surprised you didn't have one for Sammy." His gaze slid away from hers, and she wondered if he thought she wouldn't want him speaking poorly of Lloyd.

Hoping to ease his abrupt discomfort, she said, "Lloyd told me that he intended to get Sammy a cradle, but then I guess he didn't have the money for it." She ran her fingers over her belly. "This little one won't have to sleep in a drawer. *Danki*, Joshua."

Before she could think about what she was doing and halt herself, she leaned forward and kissed his cheek.

Joshua wasn't sure who was more surprised at Rebekah's kiss, him or her. She pulled back so quickly and turned away to say something to the *kinder* that he couldn't guess what she was thinking.

But he'd heard what she said. Lloyd had promised to get a cradle for their firstborn, but then hadn't given her the extraordinary one he'd purchased. Where had that cradle gone? Joshua knew it was unlikely that he'd ever get an answer. That bothered him less than the grief he'd heard in Rebekah's voice when she spoke of her late husband.

How could he hope to win her heart when it belonged to the *daed* of her two *kinder*? He hadn't relinquished his love for his late wife. Astonishment ran through him. Tildie! When was the last time he'd thought of her? He was shocked that he couldn't recall.

He went through his normal evening routine, but his gaze kept wandering to Rebekah. She worked on lengthening Levi's church pants until it was time for prayers and for the younger *kinder* to go to bed. Before she took Sammy into the downstairs bedroom, she gave Debbie and Levi each a kiss on the cheek, and his own skin sizzled with the memory of her lips against it.

Soon the footsteps upstairs disappeared as the *kinder* found their beds. Timothy had gone outside without any explanation, but Joshua was used to his son's changing moods. Not that he appreciated them, but he expected them.

When Rebekah returned, she continued her sewing while he perused a new buggy parts catalogue that had come in today's mail. Neither of them spoke as they sat facing each other across the cradle.

"Joshua, it's time," she said suddenly.

He leaped to his feet and stared at her, dropping the catalogue on the floor. "Already? I thought the *boppli* isn't due for a few more weeks. Will you be okay here while I call Beth Ann?"

She put her fingers lightly on his arm. "Joshua, it isn't time for the *boppli*. It's time to talk about selling Lloyd's farm."

Glad that the *kinder* were elsewhere so they hadn't seen him jump to conclusions, he lowered himself into his chair. He didn't wait for his heart to slow from its panicked pace as he asked, "What has changed your mind?"

"I told you I needed time to think over the decision, and I have," she said.

Joshua's teeth clenched so hard his jaw hurt. She was shutting him out again. He glared at the cradle, which had reminded her of the husband she'd chosen with love instead of the one she'd agreed to wed for convenience's sake. He'd never imagined he'd be jealous of a dead man, but he couldn't restrain the horrible emotion.

Lord, help me walk the path You have chosen for me and forget about other men's. You brought Rebekah and her family into my life for a reason. Let me be Your instrument in helping them live as You would wish for them.

"All right," he said, hoping hurt hadn't seeped into his voice. "I'll make the arrangements with Jim Zimmermann to set an auction date. It'll take some time to prepare the auction and advertise it. He'll want the most bidders there possible so you can get plenty of bids for the farm and the equipment."

"It's been this long. A little longer won't make any difference." She didn't look up from her sewing. "I'd rather not go."

"I understand," he said, even though he didn't. Actually, he comprehended why she didn't want to watch the farm as well as her house go on the block. What he didn't understand was why she'd come to the decision to sell now.

"*Gut.* Lloyd asked you to take care of us as you think best. He'd have trusted you to oversee what needs to be done, Joshua."

"Do you trust me, too?"

She finally met his eyes. *"Ja."*

His heart seemed to bounce in his chest, beating madly as if it hadn't made a sound since Tildie had drawn her last breath and it was finally coming to life again. Rebekah trusted him. As he held her steady gaze, he knew her faith in him wasn't because he'd given her the cradle and a home for her family. He saw something more in her eyes, something that spoke of respect and camaraderie. He didn't dare look for more. How could he ask for her love when he withheld his own heart? The thought of loving any woman other than Tildie seemed a betrayal.

Or was he seeing what he hoped to in Rebekah's gaze?

He would know, one way or the other, with his next words. "I'd like to talk to you about one very important matter."

"I told you. I trust you to handle the farm auction."

He shook his head. "This doesn't have anything to do with the farm. It's about Sammy and the little one."

She curved her hand over her stomach. "What about them?"

"What do you think of me adopting them?"

Her breath came out in a gasp, and she stared at him without speaking. For the second time that evening, he had shocked her into silence.

"Rebekah, I should have phrased that better. I've been thinking about this since Jeremiah dropped off the cradle. He asked if I intended to become the *kinder's* legal *daed.*"

She started to speak, then stuttered into silence again.

"Take all the time you need to consider it and pray about it, Rebekah," he said. "I'm not asking you to take this step because I want you and the *kinder* to forget Lloyd is their true *daed*, but if Jeremiah is asking, others may be, too. I think we should have an answer to give those who ask."

Finally she spoke in a whisper, "*Ja*, we should have an answer." She put the garment she'd been working on back into the mending basket and slowly stood. "I need to pray about this, Joshua."

"I will, too."

She nodded and again started to speak, but said nothing as she walked out of the room.

He heard the bedroom door softly close behind her, shutting him out as she did each night.

With a sigh, he rose. He glanced at the stairs, but how could he sleep after the evening's events? Rebekah had kissed his cheek, albeit as chastely as she did the *kinder*'s. She'd expressed her faith in him. She hadn't turned him down when he spoke of adopting her and Lloyd's *kinder*, even though he'd failed to mention the true reason why he asked. Not his brother's curiosity or anyone else's mattered as much as how much he had come to consider Sammy his own and the *boppli*, as well.

He walked into the kitchen and noticed light flowing across the floor. He looked out the window and saw two figures silhouetted against the faint light from the lantern in the barn. One was Timothy. Joshua frowned when he realized the other person was Alexis Granger. She held the handles of a large tote bag with both hands, and she was talking earnestly. He couldn't hear what they were saying, but their posture suggested they were discussing something important.

What was the *Englisch* girl doing over here at this time of night? Brad had mentioned more than once that he insisted his daughter be home by dark, except on weekend nights when she could be out until midnight with her friends.

He took a step toward the door, then heard a soft voice say, "Don't."

Turning, he discovered Rebekah coming around the kitchen table. "I thought you'd gone to bed," he said.

"Sammy wanted a drink of water, so I came to get it." She looked out the window. "If you confront Timothy in front of his friend, he won't heed anything you say. You have to talk to him as you did about working with his *onkels*. He listened to you then."

"He needs to listen to me now."

"I agree, but he won't hear you if he feels he has to defend himself. Talk to him tomorrow when you can be calm and present a reasonable argument about how he could hurt his friend's reputation if it's discovered he's meeting her after dark in the barn."

"Do you think they—"

"I think they are *gut* people who care about each other, but I don't think she sees him as anyone other than a friend. He might have a different opinion of their relationship. Even so, you've taught him well. Trust him to know the right thing to do."

He glanced once more at the teenagers, then nodded. "How do you know so much about teenagers when Sammy is only a toddler?"

"I don't know. I'm going with what my instincts tell me."

"I hope your instincts are right." He looked out to see Alexis sprinting across the yard in the direction of the Grangers' house. The large bag flapped against her legs on each step.

"So do I." He heard the fervor in her voice. "So do I."

Chapter Twelve

On the day the farm was to be auctioned, the *kinder* pleaded to attend with Joshua. Rebekah agreed because she had always enjoyed auctions. She warned them that, other than Timothy, none of them must join the crowd that was bidding unless they were with Joshua or one of their *grossmammis*. Buyers would be annoyed if they were distracted by *kinder* running about.

Grossmammi Wanda handed covered dishes to the *kinder* in the family buggy. Now that her cast was off, she seemed to be trying to make up for lost time. Each *kind*, including Sammy, was given a plate or a pot to watch over. Wanda had insisted on bringing food, even though the members of Rebekah's old district would be offering food for sale. It was a fund-raiser for a husband and wife in the district who each needed surgery.

When Joshua stepped up into the buggy, he said to his *mamm*, "We'll see you at the auction later."

"We'll be there as soon as Esther finishes frosting the cupcakes she's making." After offering a wave, Wanda climbed into her own buggy, turned it and drove down the driveway.

"I get tired trying to keep up with her," Joshua said, shaking his head. "She has more energy than a dozen people."

"True." She looked from Wanda's buggy to the one holding her family.

Sammy was giggling and trying to peek into the plastic bowl on his lap. Debbie steadied it and whispered in his ear. That set him to chortling even more. Beside them, Levi was squirming as he always did when he was excited. Timothy sat in the front with his *daed*, trying to wear an expression of world-weary boredom, though she suspected he was as eager to go to the auction as his siblings were.

They were going away for the day, and she'd be alone in the house. Sadie had gone home for the weekend, leaving food for their meals in the refrigerator. Mending waited, as always, but she didn't want to spend the day doing that or trying to work in the garden. Bending over was getting harder every day.

She wanted to spend the day with her family.

Instantly she made up her mind. "Joshua, can you wait a minute while I get my bonnet and shoes?" She smiled. "It may take more than a minute for me to find my feet and get my shoes tied, but not so long that we'll be late for the auction."

"You want to go, too?" Joshua asked.

She understood his surprise. She'd been adamant about not being there. Joshua believed it would make her sad because of memories of Lloyd. In a way, he was right, but her sorrow focused on how her dreams for a life with Lloyd had faded away into a desperate struggle to survive and protect Sammy from his *daed*.

When Joshua had asked her about adopting Sammy

and the *boppli*, he hadn't had any idea how difficult it had been not to shout out *ja* immediately. Once the *kinder* had the Stoltzfus name, they could grow up without anyone watching for Lloyd's weaknesses. Best of all, she wouldn't have to disillusion Joshua about his friend. The secret of Lloyd's abuse could truly and completely be buried along with him.

She needed to find the right time to tell him that she wanted him to be the *kinder*'s legal *daed*. A time when they were alone so the *kinder* didn't hear, and a time long enough after he first asked so he wouldn't ask the questions she didn't want to answer.

"Ja," she said. "I've changed my mind. Women do that, you know."

"So I've heard. More than once." He motioned for Timothy to move to the back with his siblings. Joshua walked with her to the house, offering to help her with her shoes, and gave her the tender smile that made her heart do jumping jacks. "I'm glad you're coming with us."

"Me, too." In fact, she couldn't remember the last time she'd been this happy. She held that close to her heart, intending to savor it through the whole day.

The sale was going well. The farm that had been quiet for so long had come alive as if a county fair had set up its midway between the house and the barns. A crowd of nearly a hundred people stood beside the recently painted barn that shone in the bright sunlight. More mingled and chatted among the buggies, wagons and cars parked in the yard and down the farm lane and out on the road. The auctioneer was making the bidders laugh with his antics as he tried to cajole a few more dollars out of them for each item.

Smoke from grills brought by the members of Rebekah's old district was laced with delicious scents of meat, peppers and onions. Rows of baked goods awaited buyers with a sweet tooth. Cans of soda and iced tea were encased in galvanized buckets of quickly melting ice.

Joshua stood to the side and watched the enthusiastic bidding for a plow that looked as if it had hardly been used. The work his brother had done to fix the buildings was going to pay dividends, he was certain, because he'd heard several groups of men discussing the value of the acreage and buildings. Their numbers were higher than his estimates. His work to arrange the machinery to its best advantage was helping each piece sell for more than he'd dared to hope. The *gut* Lord had brought generous hearts to the auction today.

He smiled as his favorite verse filled his head: *This is the day which the Lord hath made; we will rejoice and be glad in it.*

The *gut* Lord had also brought several young Amish men who were eager to set up their own farms. He recognized a few from Paradise Springs and guessed the others were from the surrounding area. Most of them worked at jobs beyond their families' farmsteads, and they longed to return to the life beloved by most plain men: husbanding God's beautiful creation. By day's end, he hoped one of them would be the new owner of Lloyd's farm, because there were a handful of *Englischers* talking about bidding on it, as well, and it was always disappointing when *gut* farmland was subdivided for another neighborhood. But, either way, the farm should sell well.

Lloyd's legacy to his wife and son and unborn *kind*.

Joshua scanned the crowd, which was intent on what the auctioneer was listing as the next lot. Where was Rebekah? He saw Levi and Debbie playing volleyball with others their age. Timothy had worked with other teens to set up a makeshift baseball diamond where abandoned hubcaps, salvaged along the road, served as bases. Home plate was simply an area scratched out in the dirt.

When the house's front door opened, Rebekah emerged with a pitcher of some fruity drink and paper cups. She went with care down the steps, and he held his breath until her feet were securely on the ground. For her to fall now could turn the *boppli* and make the delivery much more difficult and dangerous.

"Now there's a man who's in love with his wife," teased Ezra. His brother nudged him with an elbow and chuckled. "Can't keep his eyes off her."

Joshua didn't want to admit that his younger brother was right. "Don't you have better things to do than lurk around spying on me?"

"Nope." He rested his shoulder against a nearby fence post. "I've been looking for a seeder, but that one went for more than I thought it was worth. *Gut* for Rebekah, not so *gut* for me. That was what I was mainly looking for, so I need to find something to do while *Mamm* enjoys time with our neighbors."

"And Leah Beiler is here." He eyed his brother with a grin. "Are you two going to be the first to publish your marriage this fall?"

"You know better than to ask that." He chuckled.

"And that's a clumsy way of trying to divert me from noticing how you're mooning over your pretty Rebekah."

Joshua changed the subject to the work Daniel had done on the farm. That seemed to distract his brother, or perhaps Ezra was so enthralled with anything to do with agriculture that he was eager to talk about it anytime. Giving his brother half of his attention, Joshua continued to watch Rebekah.

Like his *mamm*, she was unwilling to sit while others worked. She must not overdo when she had to think of her own health and the *boppli*'s.

Ezra's laugh intruded on his thoughts. Slapping him on the arm, his brother said, "Go ahead and moon, big brother. I'll talk to you later *if* you can think of anything other than your wife." He walked away still laughing.

Joshua considered retorting, not wanting to let his brother get the last word, but what could he say? Ezra was right.

He strode across the field in the opposite direction, away from the crowd and the noise. He needed some quiet to think. He paused by the farm pond where the only noise was the chirping birds and the breeze in the reeds along the water.

Why was he trying to deny the truth? Rebekah was always in his thoughts. When he considered staying another hour at the shop to finish work, he imagined her waiting at home with his meal ready and worrying that he hadn't arrived home at his usual time. He remembered how delicate her touch had been and how she'd fretted about causing him more pain when she cleaned his cuts in the wake of the exploding root beer. Even when his *kinder* came to mind, Rebekah was there, smiling, encouraging them, scolding when necessary, loving them with an open and joyous heart.

Exactly as he longed for her to love him.

Exactly as I love her.

That thought sent a deluge through him, washing away the last remnants of his resolve never to fall in love and put his heart in danger again. Whether he turned his back on her love or tried to win it, he couldn't guarantee that he was avoiding heartbreak. But he was if he ignored the truth.

He'd fallen in love with his sweet wife, the woman he'd promised to cherish. Overwhelmed by the gift of love that God had brought twice into his life, he dropped to his knees and bowed his head as he thanked his Heavenly Father.

To that prayer he added, "Give us your blessing, too, Tildie. I know now that if I'd gone first, I would have wanted you to find someone to bring you and the *kinder* love and happiness. Please want the same for me."

A sense of peace settled upon him as he stopped fighting himself. He almost chuckled at the thought. An Amish man was supposed to play no part in any sort of war, but he'd been fighting one within himself…a futile one, because the resolution was what he'd known all along. God came into their lives and hearts through love.

He needed to remember that.

The raised voice echoed oddly through the empty house. Joshua frowned. What was going on? His *mamm* had told him that Rebekah had gone inside to get out of the hot sun. He'd expected to hear the muffled sound of the auctioneer's voice, but he heard shouts.

He strode into the living room. The room silenced, and

he looked from Rebekah who was backed into a corner, one arm protectively around Sammy and the other draping her stomach, to two men he recognized as Lloyd's brothers, Aden Ray and Milo. The latter stood too close to her, clearly trying to intimidate her. Both men stepped back and let Rebekah and Sammy rush to his side.

He urged her to take the *kind* and leave, but wasn't surprised when she shook her head. She didn't want to abandon him to deal with the two Burkholders. He took her hand and drew her closer, feeling her fingers tremble against his palm. Beside her, Sammy clung to her skirt.

"What is this?" Joshua asked in the calmest voice he could.

"Family business." Aden Ray glowered. "As Lloyd's brothers, we've got a right to a share of the profits from this farm."

"Rebekah has been generous with you already. She gave your family permission to take whatever you wanted out of the house. You did. However, the equipment and farm belong to Lloyd's son."

"Which means it goes into your pockets. How convenient for you! Marry the widow and collect the fruits of our brother's labors."

"I would have married her myself if I wasn't already married." Milo, Lloyd's older brother, sneered. "She's not bad to look at when she's not blown up like a balloon."

He stared at the man's crude, greedy smile, not dignifying the stupid comment with an answer. Tugging on Rebekah's hand and calling to Sammy, he turned on his heel to walk away.

They walked out the door. As they reached the bottom step on the front porch, his arm was seized, shocking him. He hadn't expected another Amish man to lay a hand on him in anger.

"Rebekah," he said as he drew his arm away from Milo Burkholder, "*Mamm* would like your opinion about which cakes to auction off first." That wasn't true, but he didn't want her to suffer any more of her brothers-in-law's comments. "Why don't you and Sammy find her now so they can be sold while the crowd is still large?"

She backed away, frustration and fear in her eyes that were as wide and dismayed as her son's. But anger, too, because her face had reddened, making her freckles vanish. He was astonished how much he missed them. As strong as she was in facing every challenge, the freckles softened her expressions while reminding him how gentle she was at heart. He gave her a wink, and her lips quivered before she turned and crossed the yard toward the refreshment area.

"Gut," Milo growled. "Now with her gone we can talk man-to-man."

"We don't have anything to talk about. *Englisch* law and our own traditions are clear on this. The widow and her *kinder* inherit her husband's estate. As I said, she has been very generous and offered your family everything in the house."

"It's not enough!"

"I'm sorry you feel that way, but I believe it is."

Aden Ray's hands curled into fists. As his voice rose in anger, his fists did, too. "We don't care what *you* believe! We want our share!"

Joshua couldn't believe that Lloyd's brother would actually try to strike him until the younger man swung at him. Fortunately the blow went wide. Moving out of range, he said, "We can ask our bishops to decide."

"I can make that decision on my own, and we want our share." He jabbed out with his other fist.

Again Joshua jumped away and bumped into someone. A glance over his shoulder shocked him. Timothy and several of his own brothers stood behind him. Nobody spoke, but Aden Ray lowered his fists.

This time when Joshua walked away along with his son and brothers, he wasn't stopped. He heard the Burkholders stamp in the opposite direction. Thanking his brothers, who nodded in response before they returned to the auction, he kept walking with Timothy until he had strode past most of the bidders who were so focused on the sale that, praise God, they hadn't noticed his unexpected encounter with Lloyd's brothers.

"Are you okay, *Daed*?" asked Timothy as soon as they stopped.

"I will be. This policy of always turning the other cheek is easier some days than others."

His son chuckled. "I know."

"Go and enjoy your game." As his son started to leave, Joshua called his name. He walked to Timothy and gave him a quick hug. He knew his son wouldn't allow more than that when his friends were watching. "*Danki*, son."

"Anytime, *Daed*."

"I hope not."

They laughed, and Joshua went to find Rebekah. He didn't intend to let the Burkholders—or anyone else—bully her again.

It was almost, Rebekah thought, like the night of their wedding day. The *kinder* were slumbering in the back of the buggy, including, this time, Timothy, who'd had as much fun as the younger ones at the auction. Their clothes were dotted with mustard and spots of ice cream, and she was astonished none of them had sickened from the amount of food they'd eaten.

Beside her, Joshua watched the road beyond Benny's nose. "I was glad to see the farm stay with an Amish farmer."

She smiled, recalling how one of the young women had been as giddy as a toddler with a new toy when one of the Tice boys was the highest bidder. "I hope the house and farm have many happy times for its new family."

"God willing, it will." He glanced at her as he said, "I didn't expect you'd want to stay for the sale of the farm equipment."

"Why?"

"Tildie and my sisters only watched when the lots were household items. I assumed women weren't interested in manure spreaders and plows." He grinned, his teeth shining in the streetlight they drove under. "You don't have to remind me that not all women are alike. Esther often tells me that."

"No, all women aren't alike, just as all men aren't." She relaxed against the seat and discovered his arm stretched along it. When his fingers curved down around her shoulder, she let him draw her closer.

All men were *not* alike, and she was more grateful for that truth than words could say.

His thoughts must have been the same because he said, "I didn't realize the Burkholders had such tempers."

"They do, and it doesn't take much for them to lose it." She didn't add more.

"I never saw Lloyd lose his temper."

"I know." This was the perfect opening to explain about what happened when Lloyd did fly into a rage, but she held her tongue.

Fortunately, his family had left. They discovered they couldn't gain sympathy from the crowd after word spread about how they'd stripped the house of almost everything, which was why there were no household goods for sale. She was glad to see them go.

Forgive me, Father, for not being able to forgive them for their avarice. I try to remind myself that they are a gut lesson about the importance of being generous to others. She smiled to herself, hoping God would understand her prayer was facetious. She wished the Burkholders could find the peace and happiness within themselves.

It was too nice a night to discuss Lloyd and his troublesome brothers. "Timothy seems very interested in that red-haired Yutzy girl. He was hanging on her every word when he talked to her after the ball game."

"Like *daed*, like son." He chuckled. "We find redheads catch our eyes."

She chuckled, then put her fingers to her lips, not wanting the sound to rouse the *kinder*. She glanced back to see Sammy curled up between Levi and Timothy, who had his arm protectively around the little boy.

"Thank you for a *wunderbaar* day," she whispered. "I can't remember when I've had so much fun."

"How about the time we went for a canoe ride on the pond and ended up tipping the canoe over?"

She held her breath as she did each time he mentioned a memory that contained Tildie and Lloyd. She had to choose her words with care. This time it wasn't so difficult because she had fond memories of that day, too. "Because you were being silly." She smiled. "It was a *gut* thing that we could get the mud out of our best dresses."

"*Ja*. I heard about that for a long time. Lloyd must have, too."

"That was a long time ago," she replied, not wanting to admit that she never would have dared to scold Lloyd. The next time he was drunk, he would have made her regret her words. "Joshua, I've been thinking about your adopting Sammy and the new *boppli* after it's born."

"And?" Anticipation filled his voice. "What's your answer?" He halted her from answering by saying, "Before you tell me, let me say what I should have the night I asked you. Even before your son called me *Daedi* for the first time, he'd found his way into my heart. I love to hear his laughter and watch him try to keep up with the older boys. I've dried his tears when he has fallen and scraped his knee, and I've taught him the best way I know to catch a frog down at the pond. Rebekah, even though he wasn't born as my son, in my heart it feels like he's always been my son."

She stretched to put a finger to his lips as she whispered, "I know. Don't you think I've seen how you two have grown together like two branches grafted onto the same tree?"

"So what's your answer?"

"*Ja*, I would like you to adopt my *kinder*."

He turned to look at her, his face visible in the light from the lantern on her side of the buggy. But its faint beam wasn't necessary. His smile was so broad and so bright that it seemed to glow with his happiness.

"That is *wunderbaar*," he said.

"How do we do this? I'm sure there's a lot of paper-work, but I don't know where to start."

"We'll start by asking Beth Ann."

"Why?"

His eyes twinkled like a pair of the stars glistening overhead. "Didn't you know? She has an adopted daughter."

"I didn't realize that." She thought back to the drawings that hung in Beth Ann's examination room. They obviously had been done by a *kind* because the bright colors had been created with crayons. "I'll ask her at my next appointment."

"When's that?"

"On Tuesday. If you have any questions, I'll be glad to ask her."

"I'll ask her myself. At this point, I don't think you should be driving into the village on your own."

She heard an undercurrent of anger lingering beneath his words. It halted her automatic response that she could handle matters on her own. When she thanked him, his arm drew her closer. It would be so easy to imagine them riding in a courting buggy he'd built himself, except Levi was softly snoring in the back. She shut out that sound and leaned her head against Joshua's strong shoulder.

His breath sifted through her bonnet and *kapp* as he said, "We'll keep Sammy's memories of Lloyd alive by telling him about his *daed.*"

"We don't need to worry about that now." *Or ever*, she longed to add, but if she did, then she'd have to reveal how little Joshua comprehended of the man he'd called his friend.

"*Danki*, Rebekah, for agreeing. I should have said that before."

"There is no reason to thank me. It is what's for the best for the *kinder*." She didn't add that it was the best choice for her, as well.

God, am I being selfish? I don't want Sammy to suffer any longer for the sins of his daed. *Sammy deserves to be happy and secure. And so do I.*

That last thought startled her. For so long she had listened to Lloyd telling her how worthless she was. Only her determination to remain strong for her son and her faith that God would never stop loving her as Lloyd had, had kept her from believing his cruel words.

Not tonight. She wasn't going to let the memory of Lloyd intrude tonight when she sat beside Joshua while they followed the moonlight along the otherwise deserted road. The steady clip-clop from the horse provided a rhythmic undertone to the chirps of the peepers. Lightning bugs twinkled like earthbound stars, creating flashes of light in the darkness.

It seemed too soon when they entered their driveway and came to a stop by the dark house. Beyond the trees lights glowed in the Grangers' house, but in the buggy they were enveloped in soft shadows.

"Rebekah?"

At Joshua's whisper, she looked at him. His lips brushed hers, tentative and giving her a chance to pull back. She didn't want to. His lips were warm and tasted of the fudge some of the women had been selling at the auction. Or were his lips always so sweet? She pushed that silly thought from her mind as she put her arms around his shoulders and kissed him back.

He slanted her closer to him, holding her tenderly. He

kissed her cheeks, her eyelids, her nose before finding her lips again. Her fingers sifted up through his hair, discovering it was just as soft as she'd imagined. But she'd never imagined how *wunderbaar* his kisses would be while they lit the dark corners of her heart, banishing the fear and the contempt. Joy danced through her and she melted against him.

At the sound of the *kinder* stirring in the back, he lifted his mouth from hers. She curved her fingers along his face, savoring the variety of textures. She had so many things to say, but not when the youngsters were listening.

She couldn't wait until she had a chance to tell Joshua of the state of her heart and how she had come to trust him as she hadn't thought she ever could trust any man again.

Chapter Thirteen

"Do you want us to carry those bags?" asked Debbie when the buggy stopped under the tree at the edge of the yard early the following Friday.

"I'd appreciate that." Rebekah struggled to smile as the little girl handed a bag of groceries to her brother before picking up the other one.

Last night Rebekah had been awakened by a low, steady ache near the base of her spine. Whether she shifted to her side or her back, she hadn't been able to find a comfortable position. Sleeping had been impossible, so around midnight she'd gotten up and worked on mending more of the *kinder's* clothing. It was something she could do quietly and without much light, because her fingers had guided her stitches around a hem or a patch.

Now she was so exhausted it felt as if she were wading through knee-deep mud with each step. The idea of getting out of the buggy seemed too much. All she wanted to do was crawl into bed and nap away the rest of the day and maybe tomorrow and the day after.

Nonsense! The best way to stay awake was to keep

busy. Otherwise she might not be able to sleep again tonight.

And maybe tonight there would be a chance for her and Joshua to talk. Every other evening since the auction, either he or she had been busy. Sammy had started resisting going to bed without her being there until he went to sleep. He was frightened after what he'd witnessed with Lloyd's brothers. She thanked God that her son wouldn't have to have much to do with that family from this point forward.

As she got out of the buggy, she motioned for Levi to follow his sister and Sammy into the house. "Go ahead. I'll take care of Benny and the buggy." She glanced at the clouds building up along the western horizon. "Will you ask Sadie to bring in the laundry? And please ask Debbie to cut up some of the fruit we bought and make us a salad with the berries you picked yesterday."

He nodded. She was grateful for Sadie's help because she was finding it more difficult with each passing week to hang out the wash and take it down. Last time she'd done laundry, three pieces of clothing had fallen on the grass, and she'd had to ask Sammy to collect them. It was impossible to find the basket by her feet.

Her feet? She almost laughed. She hadn't seen them in so long she doubted she'd recognize her own toes any longer.

She unhooked the horse and led Dolly toward the barn. She wasn't sure how bad the storm was going to be, and she knew Dolly didn't like getting wet. She'd put her in a stall until the rain passed. After that Levi could let the mare out into the pasture. The horse had taken a liking to the boy and vice versa.

The air in the barn was heavy. She made sure the

horse had plenty of water, and she thought about having a lovely cold glass of lemonade.

She shut the stall door and turned to leave. Sunlight glinted off something on the floor near a discarded horse blanket. She went to check, not wanting one of the horses to pick up a nail in a hoof.

She started to bend to check the shiny object, then laughed. Hadn't she been thinking that bending was impossible? Squatting was almost as difficult without something to assist her to her feet. She considered calling one of the *kinder* to help her, or she could wait until Joshua came home.

Her eyes were caught by the extra wheel leaning against the stall's wall. She could use it to help her. Checking that it would not tumble over when she grasped it, she chuckled.

"Lord, you keep me humble by reminding me that I can't do everything." She chuckled again and put her hand on the wheel. She hunkered and reached for the glistening piece of metal.

Her laughter disappeared as she realized it wasn't a piece of metal, but a metal can. Connected to five other metal cans. A six-pack of beer. A brand that must be popular among *Englischers* because she'd seen large trucks with the beer's name passing through Paradise Springs.

Her stomach heaved, and she feared she was going to throw up. Lloyd had hidden his stash of beer in the barn. Icy shudders thudded along her, battering away the happiness and contentment she had felt seconds ago.

Had Joshua hidden it here so she wouldn't suspect that he drank as Lloyd had? Her stomach twisted again. She'd thought she'd smelled liquor on Joshua's clothing while doing laundry. Since that day she'd convinced herself that she hadn't really smelled it, that it'd been her imagination or one of the lacquers Joshua used at the buggy shop.

Was this all the beer or was there more?

Rebekah shoved the six-pack under the blanket and then pushed herself to her feet. At the best speed she could manage, she went to the house, not even pausing to answer when Sadie called out a greeting. The *kinder* looked up when she came in. She rushed past where Debbie was slicing fruit and the boys were watching with eager anticipation.

"Are you looking for something?" asked Levi.

"Ja," she replied.

"Can we help?" the ever-helpful Debbie asked.

"Watch Sammy. Make sure he eats with a spoon, not his fingers. I'll be right back." She threw open the cellar door. "I need to get…" Her brain refused to work, stuck on the image of that beer in the barn. Shaking herself, she said, "I need to get a couple of bottles of your *grossmammi*'s pickles for supper."

"Let me carry them up for you." Levi stuck out his thin chest. *"Daedi* asked us to help you when Sadie is busy doing something else."

Tears flooded her eyes. She longed to put her arms around these darling *kinder* and hug them so tightly while she kept the evils of the world away from them. To do so would create more questions. Questions she couldn't answer until she had more facts. Accusing their *daed* of being as weak as Lloyd would hurt them as deeply as it had her.

"Danki, but I think I can manage. I'll call if I need

help." She hoped her smile didn't look as grotesque as it felt. *"Ja?"*

"Ja," he replied, but she didn't miss the anxious glance he shared with his sister.

Thankful that Sammy was too young to take notice of anything but his sandwich, Rebekah hurried down the stairs before one of the *kinder* could ask another question. She picked up the flashlight from the shelf by the steps and went to the shelves where fresh jars of fruit had been stored in neat precision along with the ones she's brought from Lloyd's farm. A gasp sent a pain through her. The only sanctuary she had from another alcoholic husband was that farm and now it was gone.

Why, God, did You let me discover this *after the farm was sold?* The pain burst out of her in a single, painful blast.

She couldn't blame God for a man's weaknesses. She did, however, blame herself for not seeing any signs that Joshua hid beer as Lloyd had. Even looking back over the past months, she couldn't recall a single clue that would have tipped her off. Other than that Joshua had been Lloyd's best friend, and they'd spent time together fishing and hunting. Had they been drinking together, too?

Spraying light over the shelves, she looked but didn't see anything that wasn't supposed to be there other than a few spiders. She lowered the flashlight, so the beam narrowed to a small circle on the concrete floor. There were other places where beer or a bottle of liquor could be hidden, but she couldn't squeeze past the shelves to reach them. At that thought, she aimed light through the shelves. She saw tools and what looked like cast-off furniture against the stone foundation, but everything was covered with a thick layer of dust. If it had been disturbed recently, she saw no sign.

Looking up at the ceiling, she wondered if there was a place in the attic where cans or bottles could be hidden. Lloyd had put his beer there once. A cold snap had frozen the beer and shattered the bottles, making a mess that he'd refused to clean up. She recalled the ignominy of washing the floorboards on her hands and knees while pregnant with Sammy. Rather than being grateful, Lloyd had walked out and hadn't come back for almost a week, lamenting how he'd run out of money.

Tears rolled down her cheeks. She wrapped her arms around herself and her unborn *kind*.

God, I thought Joshua was a gut *man. I dared to let him into my heart, believing that You wanted me to share his life. What do I do now?*

There was one more place to check. Lloyd often put his beer in the well house because the water stored in the tank kept it cold.

Her lower back ached more with each step she took up the stairs, but Rebekah didn't slow when she reached the kitchen. Again she was aware of the anxiety on the *kinder's* faces. She wished she could say something to comfort them, but she wouldn't lie to them.

Sadie was bringing in a basket of laundry and nearly collided with Rebekah. Waving aside the young woman's apology, Rebekah hurried around the side of the house to where the small well house contained the diesel pump and a holding tank for water. The walls were built with slats so fumes wouldn't build up inside.

After going in, she waited for her eyes to adjust. As soon as they did, she saw sunlight glinting off more metal. She leaned against the slatted walls and wrapped her arms around her belly as if she could protect her unborn *kind* from what was right in front of her eyes.

Five six-packs of beer.

She'd never seen such a collection. Lloyd seldom had had more than two or three six-packs on the farm at any one time. Or at least as far as she knew. Why would Joshua want enough beer for a dozen people?

Her eyes widened. What if the beer didn't belong to Joshua? Maybe she was jumping to conclusions about her husband. What if the cans belonged to Timothy? The teenager was so moody, leaping from cheerfulness to sullen scowls in a single breath. Lloyd had been like that, too, especially contentious when his head ached as he suffered yet another hangover.

She looked down at the six-packs. Timothy went out by himself in the family buggy on Saturday nights. How easy it would be for him to retrieve the beer and hide it beneath the backseat so even if his *daed* or another adult stopped to talk to him the beer would go unnoticed. She had no idea how many members were in his running-around gang, but she knew the gatherings often included a mix of Amish and *Englisch* teens.

So whose beer was it?

Rebekah waited impatiently for Joshua and Timothy to get home. As soon as they did, she went out into the shimmering heat to meet them. Her husband waved as he led Benny into the barn because the slow-moving storm seemed ready to pounce on them.

"Timothy," she said as the teenager started across the yard in the direction of the Grangers' house, "I need to talk with you."

"It'll have to wait. I'm already late."

"Late for what?"

He stopped and frowned. It was the expression he usually reserved for his *daed*, but she wouldn't let it halt her from saying what she must.

"Timothy, it'll take only a second."

"It'll have to wait." His voice got louder on each word until she was sure their neighbors could hear. "I'm going out with friends. I told *Daed* last night. He said it was okay for me to go out on a Friday night as long as I get my chores done tomorrow. Why are you grilling me like I'm some sort of criminal?"

Rebekah hardly considered a single question an interrogation, but her voice had been forceful. All she could think of were those cans of beer. She needed to know the truth. She'd heard about boys racing their buggies when they were intoxicated and how they ended up paralyzed or worse.

"Timothy—"

"Leave me alone!" He stamped away.

Joshua came out of the barn and looked in the direction of his son's angry voice. What was distressing Timothy *now*? When he saw his son striding away with Rebekah trying to keep up with him, he was astonished. Timothy had never raised his voice to her before. Not like this.

They stopped and his son jabbed a finger in Rebekah's direction. His gut twisted when he noticed how she didn't flinch away as she did too often when he reached toward her.

Timothy stepped back when Joshua approached. Fury twisted his son's face, and Rebekah's was long with despair.

Joshua didn't get a chance to ask what was wrong

because Timothy snapped, "She's your wife. Tell her to stop trying to run my life. She's not my *mamm*, and even if she was I'm sixteen and I don't need her poking her nose into my business." He stormed past Joshua and into the trees that divided the two houses.

Joshua started to call after him but halted when Rebekah said, "Let him go."

"Why? He owes you an apology for speaking like that."

"No, I owe him one."

Her words kept him from giving chase after his son. "Why?"

"I wanted to ask him something, and I pushed too hard. He's right. I'm not his *mamm*."

"But you are my wife. He should respect that."

"He's sixteen, Joshua."

"A *gut* reason for him to know he needs to respect his elders."

Her smile was sad, and she stared at the ground. "And there's the crux of the problem. He doesn't think of me as his elder. Oh, sometimes I'm sure he thinks I'm too old to recall what it's like to be sixteen. At other times, he thinks I'm too young to be his *mamm*. Either way, he doesn't believe I have the right to tell him what to do."

"I'll talk to him." He started to put his arm around her, but she flinched. As she had when she'd first come to live at his house. He watched in disbelief as she widened the distance between them. She hadn't acted like this since the auction. What had changed?

"I don't think it matters," she said with a sigh. "Timothy isn't going to tell me the time of day at this point Let me see if I can mend fences with him before you get involved. I don't want him to think we're siding together against him."

He nodded reluctantly. His son needed to show Rebekah respect, but trying to talk sense to Timothy when they both were upset might make matters worse in the long run. But didn't Rebekah owe him the truth, too, about why she was again acting as skittish as a doe?

He couldn't ask. Not when her color was a strained gray beneath her summer tan. He urged her to come inside and allow him to get her something cool to drink.

Maybe later she would tell him why she suddenly found his touch abhorrent.

Please, God!

A crash reverberated through the house, and Joshua sat up in bed. Rain splattered on the window, but that hadn't been thunder. It had been louder and much closer.

He leaped out of his bed and banged his head on the slanted ceiling. He rubbed the aching spot but didn't slow as he raised the shade on the window.

At the end of the driveway a car was stopped. Its lights were at an odd angle, one aiming up into the trees and the other on the grass. It couldn't be on the road any longer.

He grabbed his boots and shoved his bare feet into them. He threw open his door. When Debbie peeked sleepily out of her room, he ordered her in a whisper to go back to bed and stay there. He didn't want her to wake her brothers who were heavier sleepers. Even more important, he didn't want her to follow him out to the car in case someone was badly hurt.

His boots clumped on the stairs and he realized he should have laced up their tops to hold them on more tightly. Too late now to worry about waking up Rebekah and Sammy.

"Joshua?" he heard as he reached the bottom step.

Rebekah stood in the bedroom doorway. She wore a sweater over her nightgown. It could not reach across her distended belly, but she tugged at it.

He reached for the door. "There's a car at the end of the drive. Its lights are shining all wrong."

"A crash?"

"That's what I'm going to find out."

By the time he reached the front door, the rain was coming down hard. He grabbed an umbrella from the crock by the door. After throwing the screen door aside, he went out on the porch. He opened the umbrella and handed it to Rebekah, who had, as he'd expected, followed him from the house.

"Stay here," he ordered over a rumble of thunder.

"I'll wake Timothy."

"He may not be home yet."

Even in the darkness, he saw her face grow ashen. Her voice shook as she said, "Then I'll wake Levi. If someone is hurt, he can run to the Beilers' barn and use their phone to call an ambulance." She glanced toward their *Englisch* neighbors' house. Light glowed in the windows. "The Grangers are up. He can go there. It's closer."

He nodded, relieved that she hadn't argued about coming with him. He turned up the collar on his coat before running down the steps. The grass was slick. Flashes of lightning illuminated the sky and blinded him as darkness dropped around him and thunder boomed above him. He almost lost his footing twice on the grass, so he went toward the driveway. The gravel would be easier to run on. He saw someone moving by the bright red car. He increased his speed, but skidded to a stop when he heard a familiar voice shout for him to stop.

Right in front of him, the mailbox was sheared off. He almost had run into the sharp spikes of wood.

And his older son was leaning on the hood of the battered car.

Chapter Fourteen

Someone must have called the police, or maybe a patrol had been driving by, because they were there before Levi could go next door and call 911. One police car soon became two and an ambulance, even though Timothy insisted he wasn't badly hurt.

Rebekah had joined Joshua when the first police car arrived. A short, stocky man who introduced himself as Steven McMurray, the chief of the Paradise Springs Police Department, insisted that Timothy be checked by the EMTs. The man and woman with the ambulance kept the younger *kinder* entertained while they examined Timothy.

Joshua wished the *kinder* had remained in the house, but the rain had eased so he allowed them to watch as Timothy's blood pressure was taken and a cut on his forehead cleaned and bandaged. He was glad when they took the extra gauze and tongue depressors back to the porch to play with them.

Chief McMurray finished talking with the other officers. Joshua heard them say it was *gut* that his son had been wearing a seat belt. Even though the airbag had gone off, Timothy could have been hurt far worse than a lacerated forehead and what would probably become a pair of black eyes.

The chief worked with easy efficiency as the storm ended, leaving hot and humid air in its wake. Joshua recalled how years ago Steven had been a troublemaker along with Johnny Beiler. Now Johnny had died, and Steven was in charge of the Paradise Springs police. The Lord truly did work in mysterious ways.

Another officer handed the chief a slip of paper and spoke quietly to him. Even though he strained his ears, Joshua couldn't hear what the officer was saying.

"Maybe you should go back to the house, Rebekah," he murmured. "You are shivering."

She shook her head. "No, I'm staying."

He recognized her tone and the futility of arguing with it.

Chief McMurray walked over to them. His expression in the flashing lights from the vehicles was grim. "I wanted you to know that we ran the plates, and the car is registered to Brad Granger." He glanced along the road to their neighbor's house, then frowned at Timothy who still sat on the back bumper of the ambulance. "How did you come to have it, son?"

Timothy held an ice pack to his forehead and shrugged. "It's my friend's car, and she wouldn't care if I used it."

"Her father will care when he realizes the front end is smashed up. Taking someone else's car for a joyride with your friends is a felony."

Beside him, Rebekah gasped, knowing as Joshua did that a felony could mean time in jail.

"Who was with you?" asked Chief McMurray.

"I told you before. I was driving by myself."

The chief shook his head and frowned. "I know you teenagers think adults are stupid, but both airbags went off. The passenger side one doesn't go off unless someone is sitting there."

"Maybe it was broken."

"There's no maybe about it being a really bad idea to lie to the police. Someone most likely saw you and this car tonight. If you had someone with you, they probably saw that person, too."

Timothy blanched even paler.

"It's better for you to be honest now than later." Chief McMurray gave Timothy a chance to answer. When he didn't, the police chief looked at Joshua and Rebekah. "You also need to know that we found half a dozen empty beer cans in the car. We'd like to run a Breathalyzer on your son with your permission."

Joshua nodded, unsure if he could speak. Why hadn't Timothy heeded his warnings about the dangers of drinking and driving a buggy? His son was smart, and he should have realized that those hazards were compounded if he was behind the wheel of a car.

Beside him, Rebekah gave a sob. He started to explain the test wouldn't hurt in any way. She turned away. That surprised him. She wasn't usually squeamish.

The police administered the test, and Timothy seemed to shrink before his eyes. The cocky teenager was becoming a frightened *kind*. Every inch of Joshua wanted to comfort him, but his son had demanded the rights of an adult and now he would have to face the consequences of making stupid choices. Even knowing that, Joshua had to swallow his cheer when the test came back negative.

But if his son hadn't drank the beers, who had?

As a tow truck backed up to take the damaged car away, Chief McMurray came to where Joshua and Rebekah stood beside his son. He handed Timothy a piece of paper.

"This is a ticket for driving without a license," the police chief said. "Don't assume it's the only ticket you're going to get. Joshua, as your son is a minor, I'd like to leave him in your custody while we investigate what happened here." He ran his hand backward through his thinning hair, making it stand on end, before he put his hat on again. "I don't like to see any kid sitting in a jail cell, but I won't hesitate to put him there if I find out he took the car without permission. Do you understand?"

"*Ja,* I understand." He looked at his son, but Timothy wouldn't meet his eyes. "What happens now?"

"As he has been put in your custody, you or your wife must be with him every minute. Don't let him out of your sight. If he does something foolish like trying to sneak out, it won't look good for him when he goes before a judge. Judges, especially juvenile court judges, don't take kindly to such things. He's already in a ton of trouble. Making it worse would be foolish."

"We'll do as you ask. Is there anything else we should do?"

The chief smiled swiftly. "Pray. I know you folks are good at that."

Joshua nodded, but didn't say that he'd been praying since he'd looked out the window and seen the car lights shining at odd angles.

"*Danki,*" Rebekah said softly. "Thank you, Chief McMurray."

"You're welcome." The police chief's gaze shifted to Timothy. "I hope you're being honest when you say you had permission to drive the car." He looked back at Joshua. "We're going to be talking to the Grangers next. If they corroborate his story, I'd still like to send one of my officers over to speak with Timothy about the importance of taking driving lessons and getting his license if he intends to drive again."

"And if the Grangers disagree with what Timothy says?" Rebekah clearly was too worried to wait for Joshua to ask the same question.

"You'll have to bring him to the police station where he'll be booked for stealing a car." The chief looked from her to Joshua. "I hope we don't have to do that, but if he's lying…"

"We understand, Chief McMurray." He motioned for Rebekah to return to the house.

He thanked the policemen and the tow truck driver before he led Timothy toward the house. His son was silent. Why wasn't he apologizing and asking to be forgiven? On every step, Joshua's frustration grew.

As soon as they were inside, he ordered the younger *kinder* to their rooms. They stared at him as if they feared he'd lost his mind, because he seldom raised his voice to them.

For some reason that infuriated him more. As Levi and Debbie hurried up the stairs and Sammy grasped a handful of his *mamm*'s nightgown, Joshua spun to face his oldest and demanded, "Have you lost your mind?"

"Daed—"

"No!" he snapped. "I'll talk and you'll listen. After all, you didn't want to talk to the police. You took your friend's car and smashed it into our mailbox. You were driving a car filled with empty beer cans. Where did those come from?" He didn't give his son a chance to answer. "You act as if everyone else is to blame except you. You spin tales nobody would swallow. On one hand you expect to be treated like an adult, but then you make decisions Sammy knows better than to make."

"You don't understand, *Daed*!"

"Then help me understand. Why don't you start with why you had Alexis's car? If you don't want to start there, start with how the beer cans got into the car and who drank the beer. Don't think that I didn't understand what the police were saying. They didn't say you hadn't been drinking. Only that you hadn't drunk enough to be legally intoxicated." When he saw the tears in his son's eyes and saw bruises already forming around the bandage on his forehead, he wanted to relent. He couldn't.

He reached out to grasp his son's shoulder, hoping a physical connection would help Timothy see that Joshua truly wanted to help him. His hand never reached Timothy.

"No!" Rebekah stepped between them, batting his hand away. "Calm down, Joshua, before you do something you'll regret."

"I am not the one who needs to worry about that." He scowled at his oldest and at Rebekah. Didn't she realize what an appalling situation his son was in? Timothy could be arrested.

He took her by the arm and drew her aside. She stared at him, hurt and betrayal in her eyes. When he reached toward her again, she skittered away, wrapping her arms around herself as she had when the Burkholder brothers threatened her. Did she think he was doing *that*? He wasn't angry as much as he was frustrated.

With her, with his son, with himself for not being able to handle the rapidly deteriorating situation.

"Rebekah," he said, trying to keep his voice even. "The boy needs to realize the consequences of what he's done. Drinking and driving—"

"I didn't drink and drive!" Timothy shouted.

"Listen to him," she urged.

Looking from one to the other, he said, "Be sensible, Rebekah. Even if he wasn't drinking, he was with kids his own age who were. Kids who think they can make the rules because they know more than anyone else. I know how it goes. They start drinking together occasionally, then more often. A couple of times a week become every day. By that time, they need more and more to get the buzz they're looking for. Who knows where it'll lead?"

"I know." Her voice, though barely more than a whisper, cut through the room like the snap of a whip. More loudly, she ordered, "Don't lecture me about the dangers of alcohol, Joshua Stoltzfus! I know them too well." She held up her right hand and tapped her smallest finger. "I know how it feels when my bones are broken in a drunken rage. I know too well how a fist can shake my teeth loose and how to look through one eye when the other has swollen shut. I know what it's like to pray every night that tonight is the night my husband doesn't turn to alcohol, that tonight isn't the night his fists will harm our unborn *kind*. I know what it's like to keep all of it a secret so the shame that is my life won't ruin my son's."

"Lloyd?" he gasped. "Lloyd struck you?"

"Ja." Tears edged along her lashes, then rained down her cheeks as she said, "He loved drinking more than he

loved me. I learned that when I found out he was selling our wedding gifts to pay for his beer."

"And selling your cradle for it." Joshua wished he could take back those words as soon as he said them because he saw devastating pain flash across her face.

Her voice broke as she whispered, "My cradle? He sold the cradle he promised me for our son in order to buy himself beer?" She pressed her hands over her mouth, but a sob slipped past her fingers. Closing her eyes, she wept.

No one spoke. Even Sammy was silent as he stared at her. How much of what she'd recounted had the little boy witnessed? How much did he remember? No wonder Sammy had shied away from him at first. If the one man he should have been able to trust—his own *daedi*—had treated his *mamm* so viciously, then how could the *kind* trust any man?

How could Rebekah trust any man, either?

He watched Timothy cross the room and embrace Rebekah. She hid her face against his shoulder as sobs swept through her. Over her head, his son's eyes shot daggers at him.

None of them could pierce Joshua's heart as deeply as his own self-recriminations. How could he have failed to see the truth? He'd seen her bruises, but accepted Lloyd's excuses that she was clumsy. She wasn't clumsy. Even pregnant, she was as graceful as the swans on the pond near the shop.

He thought of the many times she'd avoided his hand when it came close to her, though he never would have raised it toward her in anger. She'd begun to trust him enough not to flinch...until today. What had changed today? He needed to ask, but how could he when he had failed her completely?

Where did he start to ask for her forgiveness?

Why didn't Joshua say something? He stood there, staring at her as Rebekah thanked Timothy for the hug. The teenager murmured that he was sorry.

"For what?" she asked. "You didn't even know Lloyd."

"I'm sorry for everything." He shuffled his foot against the rag rug, then looked at his *daed*. "I really am."

Joshua nodded and put his hand on Timothy's shoulder and gave it a squeeze, but his gaze met hers. "All I can say, Rebekah, is that I am sorry, too. I had no idea what was going on."

"I know. Nobody did."

"Why didn't you go to your bishop for help?"

She hung her head and sighed. "I tried. Once. But I didn't tell him the whole story because I knew Lloyd would be furious if he discovered what I'd done. The bishop told me to try to be a better wife. I tried, but I kept making mistakes. Lloyd would yell at me at first and then…" She glanced at Sammy. She'd already said too much in his hearing.

"You did nothing wrong. None of this was your fault."

Tears streamed down her cheeks, and she didn't bother to wipe them away. "I believed that. At the beginning. Then I began to wonder if I'd failed him in some way that caused Lloyd to drink." Her shoulders shook so hard, she wobbled.

He rushed to her side. "Rebekah, you need to sit down."

"Help me?"

"Gladly." He put his arm around her, and she leaned against him as he guided her to a chair. She wished she could always depend on his steady strength.

As Timothy took Sammy's hand, Joshua knelt beside her and put his fingers lightly over hers, which were protectively pressed to her belly. "Listen to me, Rebekah. I'm going to tell you two things that are true. If you don't believe me, ask God."

"You've never lied to me."

"And I won't. Look deep in your heart, and you'll know what I'm about to say is the truth. First, any choices Lloyd made were *his* choices. Nothing he chose to do or not do is your fault. God gives us free will, even though it must pain Him when we make bad choices." When Timothy shifted uncomfortably behind them, he didn't look at his son. His gaze remained on her. "Second, Rebekah, with our *kinder* here to witness my words, I vow to you that I will never intentionally hurt you in word or deed."

A hint of a smile touched her trembling lips as she spoke the words she had the day he asked her to marry him. "You know it isn't our way to make vows."

"Other than vows of love. Those we proclaim in front of everyone we can gather together. Before our *kinder*, I vow that I love you."

"You love me?"

"Ja, ich liebe dich." The words sounded so much sweeter in *Deitsch*, and her heart soared like a bird on a summer wind.

A loud knock sounded on the back door. Joshua rose

as Timothy tensed, fear on his face. Rebekah reached out and took the boy's hand. When he looked at her, she gave him a loving smile. If the police had returned, Timothy wouldn't have to face them alone.

When Joshua opened the door, Brad Granger stood on the other side. He was a balding man, who was wearing a plaid robe over a pair of gray flannel pants. He had on white sneakers but no socks. "May I come in?"

"*Ja*. Of course." Joshua glanced at her, but she had no more idea than he did what to expect from their neighbor.

Brad had every right to be furious if Timothy had taken the car without his permission. Their neighbor entered and called over his shoulder, "C'mon in. Lurking out there won't resolve any of this." His voice was raspy with the emotion he clearly was trying to control.

A slender form edged into the kitchen. Alexis's hair covered most of her face, but when she looked up, Rebekah could see that the girl's eye was deeply bruised, and a purplish black line followed the curve of her left cheekbone. She stared at the young girl whose face looked like reflections Rebekah had seen in her own mirror. Pain lashed her anew as she glanced at Timothy who quickly looked away. No! She didn't want to believe that the young man who had comforted her so gently had struck his friend. *Oh, please, God, don't let it be true!*

"How are you?" Timothy asked, stepping forward. She couldn't miss the concern in his words or his posture.

"It'll look worse before it looks better," Brad said with a sigh. "The EMTs who stopped by warned her that she's going to have two reasons for a headache in the morning. The bruises and a hangover." He looked at his daughter. "Go ahead. This won't get any easier if you put off doing what you should have done in the first place."

Rebekah was surprised when Alexis turned to her. "Tim thinks you found the beer in the barn."

"And the well house," she said, putting her hand on Joshua's arm when he opened his mouth to ask a question. He remained silent as she added, "I did find it. I was afraid it might belong to someone in this family, but it didn't, did it?"

"No. The beer in the barn was mine."

"Alexis—"

She interrupted Timothy with a sad smile. "You don't need to cover for me any longer, Tim. I've told my parents everything. Now I need to be honest with your folks so they know the truth."

He nodded, his shoulders sagging in obvious relief.

"I didn't think it was any big deal," the girl said, then shivered. "That is, until the police came to the house. They told me that Tim might get arrested because he took my car and crashed it. That's when I knew I had to be honest. I can't let Tim pay for my mistakes when he was simply trying to be a good friend." She took a deep breath and squared her shoulders. "I asked Tim to hide the beer so my parents wouldn't find it. I brought it over the other night and he agreed, though I could tell he didn't like the idea of deceiving our parents. Tonight I picked him and the beer up, and we went to a party out by the Conestoga River with some of my friends."

"Where you drank the beer?" Joshua asked.

"Yes. You must have seen the beer cans in the car."

She grimaced. "Chief McMurray sure did! But Tim didn't have any beer."

"I don't like it." Timothy shrugged and smiled weakly. "Tastes worse than it smells."

"I did drink some of the beer." Alexis sighed when her *daed* glared at her. "Okay, I drank a lot of the beer. Too much to drive home. Tim suggested I call my folks, but I didn't want them finding out that I'd had so much to drink. I insisted I was okay to drive home. He took my keys and wouldn't let me."

Rebekah patted Timothy's arm and said, "You did listen to your *daed* about drinking and driving."

"Hey, sometimes he's right."

Even Sammy laughed at that, though he couldn't have understood why. When he yawned, Joshua picked him up and cradled him in his arms. Rebekah's heart almost overflowed with joy at the sight of the strong man holding the little boy so gently.

Her attention was pulled back to Alexis, who was saying, "So it's true that Tim drove without a license, but he did it to keep me from driving drunk."

"And you told the police that nobody else was in the car, Timothy, because you didn't want Alexis to get into trouble," Joshua said as if he were thinking aloud. "You shouldn't have lied to the police."

"I was honest with them. I didn't say I was alone, *Daed*. I said I was driving by myself. I was because Alexis was asleep in the passenger seat, so she wasn't helping me."

"Timothy, a half truth is also a half lie."

"I know."

Alexis interjected, "If that deer hadn't jumped in

front of us, he would have gotten us home without anyone knowing the truth."

"But God had other ideas," Brad said quietly. "He was tired of Alexis's behavior and brought it out of the shadows." He turned to Timothy. "I'm sorry you were caught up in this mess, son, but thank you for being such a good friend to Alexis."

Timothy took the hand Brad held out to him and shook it. "I didn't want Alexis to risk getting kicked out of school. She has her heart set on attending the University of Pennsylvania."

Looking to where Joshua had come to stand beside Rebekah, Brad added, "You've raised a fine son, Joshua. I hate to think what might have happened if he hadn't been there tonight."

"Then don't think of it," Joshua said quietly.

Brad turned to Timothy. "The police will still want to talk with you, son, but now to confirm what Alexis has already told them."

"We will cooperate with the police." Joshua gave his son a look that said he would tolerate no more half truths.

"I know you find that uncomfortable, so I'm doubly thankful to you." Brad smiled. "Chief McMurray has assured me, Timothy, that any pending charges against you, other than the driving without a license, will be dropped. Even extenuating circumstances won't wipe out that ticket, but Alexis will be paying the fine for you."

"Danki," he said.

"No, son, thank *you* for making sure my daughter got home alive tonight."

"I'm sorry," Alexis whispered. "I hope we can still be friends, Tim."

"We'll always be friends." He glanced at his *daed*. "Just friends."

Brad and his daughter urged them to sleep well and left. As soon as the door closed, Timothy turned to Joshua.

"I am sorry about the half truths," the boy said. "Even though I thought I had a *gut* reason, I know there's never any *gut* reason to lie. I hope you can forgive me."

"I already have." He handed Sammy to Rebekah.

She took him and almost cried out as a pain cut through her back and around across her stomach. It faded as quickly as it had started, so she carried Sammy in and set him on the sofa. He curled into a ball, never waking.

Turning around, she watched Joshua put his hand on his son's shoulder. "If we expect to be forgiven, we must be forgiving. Now I must ask you to forgive me."

"For what?" Timothy asked.

"I should have given you a chance to explain. I shouldn't have jumped to conclusions."

"You didn't have far to jump. I *was* driving the car, and it's my fault it crashed."

"But it's a *daed*'s job to listen and learn if he expects his *kinder* to do the same. I'll try to do better next time, if you'll forgive me for this mistake."

"I heard a wise man once say that if we expect to be forgiven, we must be forgiving."

Joshua glanced at Rebekah, and she smiled. There were many challenges before them with their *kinder*, but she and Joshua would weather each storm as it came.

Together.

"We have to stop hiding secrets from each other," Joshua said. "Secrets don't have any place among the loving members of a family. They ended up causing us even more pain."

"I know that now, *Daed*."

Joshua looked at her.

"I know it, too." She blinked back tears. "But I couldn't bear the thought of people looking at Sammy and judging everything he does to decide if he's starting to take after his *daed*."

"No one will. They'll see that he is like his *mamm*. Generous and loving. I've said it before, but I need to say it again, because I can't keep it a secret any longer. *Ich liebe dich*."

Happiness welled up in her at his words and his loving gaze. As she reached out to take his hands, she stiffened. Pain scored her again. Harder this time. When she bent, holding her hands over her belly, she heard Joshua and Timothy ask what was wrong.

She had to wait for the pain to diminish before she could gasp, "It's the *boppli*. It's coming."

Joshua kept one arm around her as he ordered, "Timothy, go to the Grangers and use their phone." He fished a piece of paper out of his trousers. "Here is Beth Ann's number. Call her and tell her to come *now*!"

Timothy grabbed the page and ran out.

With Joshua's arm guiding her, Rebekah went to the bedroom. She reached it as another contraction began. They were coming close together. Why hadn't she had more warning? Then she realized she had. Her aching back could have been mild contractions. She'd ignored them.

After he helped her lie down on the wide bed, he said, "And I thought we'd had enough excitement tonight."

She tried to smile, but another contraction bore down on her, and she couldn't think of anything but riding its crest until it receded. She opened her eyes and saw Joshua's worried face.

"Do you think Beth Ann will get here in time?" he asked.

"I hope so." She clutched his hand. Looking up at him, she said, "I'm glad you're here, Joshua."

"I wouldn't be anywhere else."

There was so much she longed to say, to tell him how she loved him and how sorry she was to have ever believed he would treat her as Lloyd had. Gripping his hand, she focused on the *boppli*, who was coming whether the midwife was there or not.

Chapter Fifteen

The bedroom was quiet. The *kinder* were upstairs, tucked in their beds for the night. Beth Ann had finished up and left along with the doctor. Sadie would be returning in a few hours to help with the new *boppli* and take care of the household until Rebekah could manage on her own again.

Joshua put the dish towel on the rack where it could dry. Taking a deep breath, he yawned as he gazed out the window. The moon had set, and the stars were a glittering tapestry of God's glory. To the east, a thin, gray line announced the coming of a new day.

The day another *kind* had joined their family.

This is the day which the Lord hath made; we will rejoice and be glad in it. His favorite verse echoed in his mind, this time a praise instead of an urging to get through yet another day while weighed down with grief.

Wanting to see the little one again, because it had been so long since there had been a *boppli* in the house, Joshua tiptoed into the downstairs bedroom to make sure *mamm* and *boppli* were doing well.

Despite his efforts to be quiet as he edged around the

bed, Rebekah's eyes blinked open. With her magnificent red hair scattered across the pillows and a joyful smile warming her lips, she was more beautiful than he'd imagined. She held out a hand to him.

Sitting on the very edge of the bed, he asked, "How are you doing?"

"Happy."

"*Ja*, I know." He didn't say any more. There wasn't any need.

The night had begun as a nightmare. One that left his hands shaking whenever he thought of what could have happened when his inexperienced son had driven that powerful car along the twisting, hilly road. It had ended with healing between him and his oldest, as well as the appearance of his youngest.

At that thought, he reached down into the cradle Jeremiah had made and lifted out a swaddled bundle.

"She is sweet," he said. "Debbie is going to be so pleased to have a sister."

"Wanda Almina Stoltzfus," Rebekah murmured. "Welcome to the world."

He handed the *boppli* to her. "*Mamm* will be pleased that you want to name this little one in her honor."

"I was named for my *grossmammi*, and I loved having that connection. Little Wanda will have that same connection with your *mamm* and mine."

"A very special gift for her very first birthday."

"I'm glad you think so." She looked from the beautiful *boppli* to him. "*Danki* for being here, Joshua."

"Where else would I be when our *boppli* was being born?"

"Our *boppli*," she whispered.

"I cannot think of her any other way. I am blessed to

have three sons and two daughters." He chuckled. "They make me *ab in kopp* way too often, but I am even crazier in love with you." He became serious. "I told you that earlier tonight how I love you. Do you love me?"

"*Ja*. Looking back, I think I started falling in love with you the day you came with your nervous proposal." She laced her fingers through his much wider ones. "At first I tried to stop myself because I knew you still loved Tildie."

"But—"

"Let me say this, Joshua." When he nodded, she continued. "I knew that you still love Tildie, and I thought there was no place in your heart for me. It took me far too long to realize that our hearts can expand to love many people. Timothy, Levi and Debbie hold a place in my heart as surely as if I had given birth to them. I see you with Sammy and Wanda, and I know you'll be a devoted and loving *daed* for them." She laughed. "Look how far my heart has expanded to welcome your *mamm*, your six brothers, your two sisters and the rest of your family. I'm blessed that there's no limit to the number of people a heart will hold."

"As long as there's always a place for me."

"There always will be."

He gently kissed her lips, knowing she was spent after the night's events. There would be plenty of opportunities in the future to kiss her more deeply, and, as Rebekah Mast Burkholder Stoltzfus's husband, he didn't intend to let a single one pass them by.

* * * * *

Dear Reader,

Welcome back to Paradise Springs…and greetings if this is your first visit. I like to read (and to write) about strong women, especially those who live their lives with quiet courage. When I decided to write about a woman who had survived a marriage to a weak man, I knew I wanted her to have a chance for a joy-filled life with a man whose spirit and faith were as strong as hers. I hope you have enjoyed reading their story of perseverance in the search for a happy-ever-after ending as much as I did writing it.

Stop in and visit me at www.joannbrownbooks.com Look for my next book in the Amish Hearts series coming soon from Love Inspired.

Wishing you many blessings,
Jo Ann Brown

REQUEST YOUR FREE BOOKS!

2 FREE INSPIRATIONAL NOVELS
PLUS 2
FREE
MYSTERY GIFTS

Love Inspired®

YES! Please send me 2 FREE Love Inspired® novels and my 2 FREE mystery gifts (gifts are worth about $10). After receiving them, if I don't wish to receive any more books, I can return the shipping statement marked "cancel." If I don't cancel, I will receive 6 brand-new novels every month and be billed just $4.99 per book in the U.S. or $5.49 per book in Canada. That's a saving of at least 17% off the cover price. It's quite a bargain! Shipping and handling is just 50¢ per book in the U.S. and 75¢ per book in Canada.* I understand that accepting the 2 free books and gifts places me under no obligation to buy anything. I can always return a shipment and cancel at any time. Even if I never buy another book, the two free books and gifts are mine to keep forever.

105/305 IDN GH5P

Name _____ (PLEASE PRINT) _____

Address _____ Apt. # _____

City _____ State/Prov. _____ Zip/Postal Code _____

Signature (if under 18, a parent or guardian must sign)

Mail to the **Reader Service:**
IN U.S.A.: P.O. Box 1867, Buffalo, NY 14240-1867
IN CANADA: P.O. Box 609, Fort Erie, Ontario L2A 5X3

Are you a subscriber to Love Inspired® books and want to receive the larger-print edition?
Call 1-800-873-8635 or visit www.ReaderService.com.

* Terms and prices subject to change without notice. Prices do not include applicable taxes. Sales tax applicable in N.Y. Canadian residents will be charged applicable taxes. Offer not valid in Quebec. This offer is limited to one order per household. Not valid for current subscribers to Love Inspired books. All orders subject to credit approval. Credit or debit balances in a customer's account(s) may be offset by any other outstanding balance owed by or to the customer. Please allow 4 to 6 weeks for delivery. Offer available while quantities last.

Your Privacy—The Reader Service is committed to protecting your privacy. Our Privacy Policy is available online at www.ReaderService.com or upon request from the Reader Service.

We make a portion of our mailing list available to reputable third parties that offer products we believe may interest you. If you prefer that we not exchange your name with third parties, or if you wish to clarify or modify your communication preferences, please visit us at www.ReaderService.com/consumerschoice or write to us at Reader Service Preference Service, P.O. Box 9062, Buffalo, NY 14240-9062. Include your complete name and address.

LI

When Kayla had discovered she had a bodyguard, she hadn't expected this. He should be in the background, quietly observing. Her father was a lawyer and a politician; she'd seen bodyguards and knew how they did their jobs. And yet here she sat with this family, her bodyguard talking of cattle and fixing fence as his sisters tried to cajole him into taking them to look at a pair of horses owned by Kayla's brother.

A hand settled on her back. She glanced at the man next to her, his dark eyes crinkled at the corners and his mouth quirked, revealing a dimple in his left cheek.

Boone opened his mouth as if to say something but a heavy knock on the front door interrupted. He pushed away from the table and gave them all an apologetic look.

"I think I'll get that." His gaze landed on Kayla. "You stay right where you are until I say otherwise."

"They wouldn't come here," she said. And she'd meant to sound strong; instead it came out like a question.

"We don't know what they would or wouldn't do, because we don't know who they are. Stay." Boone walked away, his brother Jase getting up and going after him.

Kayla avoided looking at his family, who still remained at the table. Conversation had of course ended. She knew they were looking at her. She knew that she had invaded their life.

And she knew that her bodyguard might seem like a relaxed cowboy, but he wasn't. He was the man standing between her and the unknown.

Don't miss
HER RANCHER BODYGUARD
by Brenda Minton, available June 2016 wherever
Love Inspired® books and ebooks are sold.

www.LoveInspired.com

"Make another move, and I'll shoot you where you
stand…" He trailed off, jaw sagging. Had he entered the
wrong house?

"Don't shoot! I can explain! I—I have a letter. From
Will Canfield." A petite dark-haired woman standing on the
other side of his table lifted an envelope in silent entreaty.

At the mention of his friend's name, he slowly lowered
his weapon. But his defensive instincts still surged
through him. When he didn't speak, she gestured limply
to the ornate leather trunks stacked on either side of his
bedroom door. "Mr. Canfield was supposed to meet us at
the station. His porter arrived in his stead… Simon was
his name. He said something about a posse and outlaws."
A delicate shudder shook her frame. "He said you
wouldn't mind if we brought these inside. I do apologize
for invading your home like this, but I had no idea when
you would return, and it is June out there."

Her gaze roamed his face, her light brown eyes
widening ever so slightly as they encountered his scars.
It was like this every time. He braced himself for the

inevitable disgust. Pity. Revulsion. Told himself again it didn't matter.

When her expression reflected nothing more than curiosity, irrational anger flooded him.

"What are you doing in my home?" he snapped. "How do you know Will?"

"I'm Constance Miller. I'm the bride Mr. Canfield sent for."

"Will's already got a wife."

Pink kissed her cheekbones. "Not for him. For you."

His throat closed. He wouldn't have.

"I was summoned to Cowboy Creek to be your bride. Your friend didn't tell you." A sharp crease brought her brows together.

"I'm afraid not." Slipping off his worn Stetson, Noah hooked it on the chair and dipped his head toward the crumpled parchment. "May I?"

Miss Miller didn't appear inclined to approach him, so he laid his gun on the mantel and crossed to the square table. He took the envelope she extended across to him and slipped the letter free. The handwriting was unmistakable. Heat climbed up his neck as he read the description of himself. He stuffed it back inside and tossed it onto the tabletop. "I'm afraid you've come all the way out here for nothing. The trip was a waste, Miss Miller. I am not, nor will I ever be, in the market for a bride."

Don't miss
BRIDE BY ARRANGEMENT
by Karen Kirst, available June 2016 wherever
Love Inspired® Historical books and ebooks are sold.

www.LoveInspired.com

LIHEXP05